HIS NAME WAS EZRA

CRAIG MOODY

Visit us at: www.vividimagerypublishing.com

Vivid Imagery Publishing
www.vividimagerypublishing.com

Vivid Imagery Publishing print and digital first edition January 2018

Vivid Imagery Publishing books may be purchased in bulk for educational,
business, fund-raising, or sales promotional use. For information, please
e-mail Promotions@vividimagerypublishing.com.

Publishers Note: This book is a work of fiction. Any references to historical
events, real people, or real places are used fictitiously. Other names,
characters, places, and events are products of the author's imagination, and
any esemblance to actual events or places or persons, living or dead, is
entirely coincidental.

Cover art illustration and design by Evgeniya Hitz
Edited by Stacey Kopp

Printed in the United States of America
ISBN 978-0-9986558-8-8 (Hardcover)
ISBN 978-0-9986558-5-7 (Paperback)
ISBN 978-0-9986558-6-4 (Kindle)
ISBN 978-0-9986558-7-1 (eBook)

*Dedicated to my Aunt Judy and my Aunt Penny:
my two red-headed angels.*

*In memory of Emmett Till, and every person of
color whose life was cut tragically short and their
murderers unprosecuted due to the brutality and
injustice of the Jim Crow South.*

HIS NAME WAS EZRA

Part I

Waynesboro, Mississippi
1957

1

His Name Was Ezra

His name was Ezra, dark eyes, skin the hue of milk chocolate, lips as pink and full as a spring meadow's first blooming rose. His smile, hypnotic; a voice that could rival the unmistakable boom of summer thunder. His eyes twinkled whenever he spoke, his soft pink lips glistening in a dew of gentle perspiration. His hair, a carefully maintained coif, reminiscent of Clark Kent's, gleamed atop his head as a genetic badge of honor. My heart fluttered as he playfully spoke my name, the sound of the word joining the constant song of the buzzing cicadas.

My name is Judith, though Ezra called me "Judy-Bee," either because my last name is Bracewell or because I somehow reminded him of a stinging insect. My hair, auburn, the color of fresh turmeric; my skin as white as dough. A celestial-like pattern of freckles adorns my cheeks, a pink shield of crimson blanketing their orbit.

I had met Ezra three years prior, our paths crossing in the acreage of endless woods behind my house. That was junior year, the realization that I was in love with him solidifying just prior to graduation.

Ezra loved me too, though he never dared to say it. We would meet in secret in an abandoned Civil War-era cemetery about a quarter mile deep in the woods, our shared time forbidden, our natural bond sinful by the laws of Jim Crow.

"Ya really know howta hit that ball, Miss Judy-Bee. I ain't neva' seen a man hit it that hard, much less a pretty female."

Ezra's words were warm and smooth as he spoke, his face brilliant with the glow of enthusiasm.

"I told ya a girl can hit," I replied in a playful boast of confidence. "I been playin' baseball with my brotha since I was in kindergarten. I know I can hit betta' than any man I eva' seen."

"That may be the truth, Miss Judy-Bee. Ya certainly hit harda' than any'a the fellas I eva' knowed."

His eyes glistened with mischief as he turned to meet my gaze. "Well, 'cept for me, a'course."

I jabbed his side as he fell into a fit of his own laughter. My heart lost its rhythm as I watched his eyes close at the mercy of his authentic and infectious joy. Whenever I was with Ezra, all time ceased and all cares and worries slipped from my mind like grain from a wounded satchel.

The conversation continued as we journeyed the path leading from the Negro side of town and into the woods. My presence here was forbidden, not to mention dangerous, but I never cared. I eagerly and openly joined a group of black boys for a game of baseball nearly every Saturday evening. As soon as my shift was up at Dolsan's Grocery in the heart of Waynesboro, I would disappear into the woods behind the house I shared with my two siblings, a younger sister named Francis and our older brother, Ed. Our daddy had long passed; I was only five when it happened. Momma had gone off a few years later and remarried in Biloxi, leaving her two young-adult children to fend for themselves.

Luckily, the house was paid for; a wood-framed single-room cottage that bordered the very edge of Wayne County. The only thing that stood between our house and the Alabama state line was a vast stretch of woods and the colored section of town.

"Ya eva' think to try out for the All-American Girls Baseball League?" Ezra asked as he jumped atop the badly crumbled tomb we favored in the tiny, long-forgotten graveyard. As kids, my siblings and I found this relic of a cemetery far too terrifying to even venture near, much less go inside of, but as an adult white woman, it was the only safe place where I could sit and spend time with Ezra.

"Ah, nah," I answered, allowing Ezra to pull me next to him from the ground. I never needed his assistance, yet I always obliged when he offered.

"Well, I really think ya should, Miss Judy-Bee. I heard on the radio they be havin' they spring trainin' down in Pascagoula next year. Ya oughta go down and see if ya can try out."

I stared at Ezra for a long moment, lost in the authenticity of his support of me. No other person in my life, much less a male, ever encouraged my ball playing. Most others just urged me to hurry on and find a husband, pop out a few youngins, and perhaps start a tomato garden. Ezra was the only soul who recognized how much I loved baseball.

"Well, a'course I know all about the Girls League. It's been my dream to play for 'em since the war. It'd neva' happen though. I got too much I gotta tend to around here."

"Like what?" Ezra questioned, his eyes steady and focused on mine. "What's more important than followin' ya dream, Miss Judy-Bee?"

I wasn't certain how to fathom a response. For a black man, Ezra viewed the world with the most unlimited and untainted perspective. He often spoke of lofty goals and passions. He had once told me he hoped to go to law school one day, a dream we both knew was difficult, if not impossible, to achieve in Mississippi. Still, I humored his ramblings of sincere delusion, even asking what color wallpaper he'd hang in his law office once he started to practice.

"Ezra," I began, brushing away an interested horsefly from my arm, "a small-town girl like me ain't got no place in a professional league. I do mighty fine keepin' my place right here, playin' ball with you boys on Saturdays."

I could feel Ezra's eyes burning into the side of my face as I spoke. I could feel his anger and disappointment billowing around me like a summer storm reaching for the heavens.

"Besides, I ain't got no money to be aimlessly runnin' around Mississippi. I'm tryin' to save what I can now to hopefully buy myself a car in the near future."

I lifted my gaze to his, the sparkle of his eyes reflecting my face back at me in the soft light of the setting sun.

"I don't wanna haveta depend on some man to drive me around. I wanna be able to come and go as I please and as I needta."

"I hear ya, Miss Judy-Bee. But I can't say I feel ya."

"What's that s'posed ta mean?" I asked, slapping another horsefly from my flesh.

"I just sayin'," Ezra replied, nervously snapping a twig with his fingers. "All we got is this one set life the Good Lord gave us. I just think it's a shame to live it without doin' somethin' special."

He lifted his face toward the dimming daylight, his expression softening under the faint glimmer of the evening stars.

"I believe ya could do it, Miss Judy-Bee," he replied after a long moment of self-reflection. "Ya good, and I ain't just sayin' that 'cause I know ya." He dropped his star-filled gaze back to mine. "I believe it 'cause I believe in ya."

I couldn't breathe for a moment as I heard his words fill the space around us. Gone were the decaying graves of a better-off-forgotten era of history, gone the endless hum of the cicadas, and gone the humid-thick air of the Mississippi night. All I could see was Ezra, his honest words seeming to fuel the beat of my heart and fill the air of my lungs. Somewhere in the moment, I slipped my fingers over his. I watched as his eyes widened, his focus dropping to the intermingling of our skin.

"Miss Judy-Bee," he whispered, the sound of his voice becoming innocent and childlike.

"Kiss me, Ezra," I whispered back, tightening my grip over his.

He darted his eyes from our hands and into the distance around us, a nervous veil of uncertainty clouding his expression.

"I . . . uh . . . I'm . . ." his words dropped from his tongue and into the dry leaves below us like acorns from a live oak tree.

I pressed my face to his, our lips touching for the very first time. I had long fantasized of this moment, dreaming of it more nights than I could ever possibly imagine counting. For whatever reason, the moment felt right, the timing aligned, and my state of mind suddenly certain and brave. I could feel Ezra tremble in the ever-so-slight distance between us. I lifted my hand to grip his face, when he stopped me.

"Judy . . ." he whispered, the first time in years he forgot the "Bee." "Ya know this ain't right."

I pulled away, the shadows of the fast-approaching night darkening their grip around his face.

"What ain't right, Ezra?" I questioned, awkwardly shifting my weight away from him.

He looked around again, his energy more intense and heavy than before.

"We . . . us . . ."

His words faded beneath the groaning night bugs. I felt my eyes water in embarrassment.

"I'm sorry, Miss Judy-Bee. I just . . . I just don't . . ."

"It's fine, Ezra."

I looked away, my dripping tears rivaling the warmth of the thickness of air around us.

"I understand."

With that, I jumped from the tomb and began to make my way toward the broken iron gate that provided the sole entrance to the cemetery. In my frustration, the corner of my cotton skirt snagged the edge of a sharp tombstone that lay beside the gate. Ezra freed me before I had the chance to reach for the garment.

"Ya don't understand, Miss Judy-Bee," he said, awkwardly fumbling his hands together.

"But I do, Ezra. I promise ya, I do."

I turned to face the gate, anticipating another interruption from Ezra, but there wasn't one. Using only the flickering candle of memory, I trampled through the trees until the quaint site of my house broke through the thickness of brush. I didn't turn back to see if Ezra had followed me; I simply rounded the side of the house and bounded the worn-out steps of the front porch in a silent and methodic trance. I didn't want to think or imagine anymore. All I wanted was to fall into bed and never wake, the weight of my sudden shame and embarrassment as cumbersome as the heavy front door of the house.

The smell of my sister's cooking greeted my nostrils as I entered the single room of the cottage. I kept my eyes down as I headed for the curtain which separated Francis's and my bed from Ed's. I dropped onto the faded quilt and pillows without saying a word to Francis.

"Well, hello to you too, Big Sista," Francis shouted from the kitchen. "It's so nice to see ya. Yes, yes, I did have a good day. Thank ya for askin'."

Sighing, I rolled myself from the bed and returned to the main room of the house. My sister smiled coyly as I neared her.

"What's the matta', Judy? Not enough excitement for ya today down at Dolsan's?"

I cracked a smile as I heaved open the icebox. Retrieving the glass milk carafe, I turned toward my sister and nodded at the bubbling contents on the stove.

"What's that?" I asked, attempting to contain the weight of my true emotion.

"Green peas," Francis replied, following my gaze to the scratched and worn sole iron pot on the stove.

"Oh, *green* peas?" I questioned playfully. "Thank God they ain't purple peas."

Francis rolled her eyes as she brought her beaming blue stare back to mine. I often admired my sister's natural beauty. Unlike mine, her face wasn't plagued by the distraction of blemishes or freckles. Instead, her skin glowed like the face of the sun itself, golden and shimmering, her brilliant, large blue eyes appearing like bottomless pools hidden someplace deep within the Amazon. Granted, Francis cared far more over her appearance than I ever did my own. Despite what many of the boys in town would say, I didn't see myself as any sort of beauty, most certainly not in the same way as my sister, Francis. The girl would spend countless hours just brushing her hair, polishing her nails, powdering her face, staining her lips. Once I was bathed, I dressed, pulled my hair into a bun, and went about my business. Francis, on the other hand, prepared for each and every day as though the man of her dreams would most certainly be arriving. At just seventeen, she was far more physically developed and wise for her own good. As our momma used to say, "Judy, ya got the brains a man needs in his life, but ya sister, well, Francis got the bosom that'll cause 'em to sin."

I couldn't say I was ever really envious of my sister, more amused by the effort she made at pleasing boys.

"Billy Jennings came by an hour or so ago," Francis announced, returning to the peas for one last stir before draining them into a strainer. "He's back in town for Easta', lookin' after his granny again."

I took a seat at the cherry wood kitchen table, the one and only piece of furniture in the house that held any sort of notable value. Daddy had saved and bought it for Momma as a wedding gift. They already had Ed by then, so Daddy had worked two jobs just to keep food on the table. He bought the house from an estate auction, the cottage once a part of a large and profitable farm that fell into decay when the original family who had owned it slowly passed on or moved away. Momma remained with us for nearly a decade before she met her husband, Jackson, and moved to Biloxi. I was happy for Momma. She was never quite right after Daddy died, and though I was so young when he passed, I did have a few select memories of my momma before her depression fully seeped in. Even when she married Jackson, I knew the lock of her broken heart hadn't loosened its grip. If anything, it only tightened.

"Anyway," Francis continued, propping open the creaking oven door for a peek at the small roast within. My mouth watered a bit as the aroma of the succulent meat filled the space of the small house. "I told Billy you was still workin', but he said he had already been down to Dolsan's to see ya."

I looked up to see my sister now eyeing me suspiciously.

"But he said ya wasn't there. Mr. Dolsan told him ya had finished ya shift around two hours earlia'."

I watched in silence as my only sister slowly moved her eyes over my face like an inquisitive yet knowing mother.

"So, where were ya, Judy?"

The sudden and unexpected question seized my heart and gripped my throat, several long seconds passing before I could summon the courage of a lie.

"Well, damn!" a male voice thundered through the house. "That's gotta be the smell of my baby sista's world-famous pot roast!"

Francis and I turned our heads to see our older brother, Ed, removing his ballcap and glasses. His face, though only twenty-three years old, appeared aged and haggard in the dim light of the solo bulb of the kitchen. His hands, blackened with dirt and debris, smeared over his denim coveralls as he ventured into the kitchen near Francis.

"Hey, Baby Sis," he chimed in a singsong voice, planting a loud kiss on Francis's forehead.

"Hey, Brotha. Don't even think about openin' that oven! You'll dry out my roast!"

I watched from the table as my two siblings playfully bickered in front of the exhausted kitchen range. I closed my eyes and sighed in relief that my brother's arrival home had interrupted my sister's line of questioning. Still, knowing Francis, it would only be a matter of time before she brought the subject back up again. I began to stir a series of lies in my head, when Francis called my name.

"If ya don't mind liftin' a finga', dear Sista, it'd be nice if ya could set the table."

I lifted my weight from the solid wood chair and shuffled into the kitchen.

"Oh, I don't know," I replied, hunching my back to mimic an elderly woman. "As the elder sista, I'm far too fragile to handle such a chore."

Francis rolled her eyes as Ed cackled from behind her. I grabbed the only three plates we owned and a set of forks before making my way back to the table. Ed followed me.

"So, Sis, I saw Billy Jennings out in town today," he blurted as he wiped his hands with a rag. "Said he might come by to see ya."

I peered at Francis from the corner of my eye, grateful that her attention was fully attuned to the glimmering roast inside the small oven.

"Uh," I choked, swallowing a dry lump of unexpected nervousness. "Yeah, I heard he was back in town. I'm sure I'll catch up with him at some point."

I caught my brother's eyes as he concluded his hand wiping and moved to his place at the head of the small kitchen table.

"Ya know, Sis," he spoke in a sigh as he allowed the full weight of his body to surrender to the chair. "Ol' Billy boy comes from a whole lotta money. His daddy is the attorney general of Mississippi. Ya'd be a smart lil' lady to keep his fancy."

I lowered my head, elongating the process of maneuvering chipped porcelain dishes and bent silverware over the small round table.

"I'd give anything for Billy Jennings to tickle my fancy," Francis announced as she neared the table, her oven-mitt-covered hands pridefully presenting a picture-perfect roast. "Dinna', my family, is served."

Both Ed and I folded our lips at the watering of our mouths as Francis lowered the gorgeous entree onto the center of the table. Taking a brief moment to admire her masterpiece, Francis smirked and spun on her heels to retrieve the waiting bowl of peas.

I took my seat at the opposite end of Ed just as Francis returned to the table.

"But," she continued, plopping a dab of peas onto a plate, "Sista girl here doesn't seem to have much interest in fine, rich, beautiful Mr. Jennings."

I kept my eyes fixed on the work of her hands as she spoke, too annoyed and embarrassed to give her the satisfaction of my expression.

"I woulda married that man and had three'a his babies at this point if I was you."

She concluded her crass statement by presenting a plate before my starving presence. I lifted my fork and began to jab at the tender meat in silence.

"I don't get it," I heard Ed pipe in from across the table. "Why don't ya give ol' Billy a chance, Judy?"

I sighed, realizing I was not going to be able to escape the awkward and unpleasant interrogation of both my brother and sister, so I lifted my face toward their gawking expressions.

"It's not that I don't give Billy a chance," I started, nervously twisting another morsel of meat with my fork. "It's just . . . he . . . he lives too far from here."

Both siblings burst into their own fits of laughter.

"Girl, ya such a fool!" Francis declared as she seated herself in her chair. "Ya twenty-one years old, Judith! Ya could marry that boy and live in luxury. His daddy would make sure ya two had everything ya needed as Billy completes school. Ya know he's nearly outta law school. With his daddy the state attorney general, some say little Billy is destined to be state governa'."

I dropped my eyes back to my plate, completely and utterly irritated by the very mention of Billy Jennings. William, Bill, or Billy, as he was better known, had been attempting to gain my attention since my senior year of high school. He wasn't from Waynesboro; born in Jackson, he had attended a boarding school for boys in Meridian, only returning to Waynesboro to visit, and now temporarily care for, his ailing grandmother, Elie Jennings. Widow Jennings lived in the biggest house in Waynesboro. Her dearly departed husband of just over sixty years had been the wealthiest and most influential landowner in the county. After his death, five or so years ago, Elie refused to leave the house she had shared with her husband to reside with her only son and daughter-in-law in their elegant home in the state capital. Growing up, we saw Billy Jennings around town every summer, but he didn't become interested in me until my last few months of high school. Thankfully, he spent most of his time attending the University of Mississippi School of Law, a hundred or so miles to the west. There wasn't anything the matter with Billy Jennings. I had no reason not to like him. In fact, he was most girls' idea of a dream man. He was tall, athletic, and very good-looking. He had graduated at the top of his class and was nearly through with law school, with a very promising legal and political career in his future. Still, my heart desired only one man, and though my mind knew the limits and reality of such a bond, my heart did not acknowledge nor honor any such boundaries. I humored Billy whenever he politely tried to flirt with me, but all along, in my head, I only thought of Ezra. I was careful not to disrespect the purity of my feelings for him by giving Billy Jennings too much of my attention. After the event of earlier this evening with Ezra, Billy was certainly the very last person I cared or needed to see at this point.

"Well, I'll be damned," Ed declared, a smirk emblazoned across his face as he focused on the small kitchen window. "Speakin' a' ol' Billy boy, I hope ya ready to see him now, Judy, 'cause he just pulled up."

My heart sank into my core as I struggled to catch my breath. A nervous pang of terror struck through my body as I understood the reality I was soon to face. Slowly, I stood from my chair and made my way to the front door, the overzealous expressions of interest and curiosity of my two siblings following my every step.

I stood still before the door, dreading each second as I awaited the certain knock.

"Perhaps it's a sign, Sista," I heard Francis exclaim in the background. "We conjured up what is meant to be just by speakin' his name."

The sound of Billy's knocking silenced the room. A wave of irritation flowed into the pool of fear and annoyance that already filled my core. Sucking in a mouthful of air, I closed my eyes and heaved the heavy door open.

"Hey, Judith." Billy smiled from the other side of the threshold. "I've been lookin' for ya."

I cracked a smile, allowing my eyes to trail into the dimly lit distance behind him. Like a ruby lost in the muck, the front of Billy's grandma's maroon 1950 Ford Coupe shimmered in the soft light from the kitchen window. I lifted my eyes to meet Billy's.

"I heard," I murmured, my voice carried off by the insect-led symphony of the Mississippi night.

"I'm back in town for a few weeks. Here to stay with Granny till next semesta' starts up."

I smiled, nodding my head in pretend interest. A part of me wanted to slam the door in his face and just return to my dinner, but I pressed forth with the situation as any genteel and polite Southern girl would.

"That's nice, Billy. How is ya granny these days?"

Billy's eyes sparkled at the mention of his grandmother. Where many boys could be considered a "momma's boy," Billy was a bona fide "grandma's boy." As far as he was concerned, the sun and moon rose and set just for the likes of Elie Jennings. The woman could probably convince her grandson to commit a murder, a sin he would oblige without regard or question, simply because his beloved granny commanded it of him.

"She's good," Billy replied, his boyish good looks evident even in the faint light of the front porch. "She's havin' a bit'a trouble gettin' around real good, but otha' than that, she's her usual fiery self."

I continued to smile, Billy's words falling around my ears as hollow and empty as the dry, falling leaves in autumn. I turned my head to see my sister and brother, both beaming from the kitchen table like marquee bulbs. I glared at them disapprovingly as I verbally responded to Billy.

"That's good to hear, Billy. Ya granny is an asset to this town. I'm gladta hear she's doin' so well."

I kept my eyes locked on my family as I spoke, my words buoyant and concerned, but my eyes bored and annoyed.

"Well, Billy," I continued, returning my face toward his, "I appreciate ya stoppin' by, but if ya don't mind, I need to return to my dinna'."

"Oh, don't send him away!" Francis called from the kitchen table. "We have enough here for another hungry belly. Come on, Sista, invite Billy in for some dinna'."

My eyes remained fixed on Billy, my smile causing my cheeks to ache in defiance to the forced expression.

Billy's face lit up at my sister's invitation, but he hesitated as I stood before him in silence. Realizing there was no way out of the growing momentum of the Billy visit, I stepped to the side, the waft of Billy's aftershave greeting my nostrils as he passed me.

I shut the door as the sound of my siblings greeting Billy filled the space of the small cottage. I closed my eyes and leaned against the door, sighing in defeat, yet absorbing my genteel composure with another mouthful of air. I returned to the table just as my sister presented a beaming Billy with a plateful of roast and peas.

Billy smiled at me coyly as I took my seat. I smiled back, my teeth clenched in pain in an effort to uphold the curvature of my lips.

Throughout the hour-long meal, I chimed in here and there to the conversation, but my head and interest were most certainly nowhere near the core of the mindless chatter. I felt Billy's foot tap mine a time or two, a subtle attempt to initiate a flirtatious game of footsie, but I ignored him.

Alone on the front porch, I allowed Billy to kiss my cheek as he said his goodbye. I agreed to let him escort me home after my shift tomorrow evening. I felt I had no other choice and hoped the extended attention would appease his interest for a while. All in all, my heart ached that my uncertain exit from Ezra earlier this evening would have to be left unresolved until further notice. Perhaps giving it a day or two to settle would be for the best.

I smiled and waved as Billy skidded his granny's Ford down the gravel pathway that led from our house to the main road. Back inside the kitchen, I silently assisted Francis with the after-dinner cleanup while she rattled my ear off with her senseless gossip and chatter.

Lying beside her a few hours later, I drifted into the dream world, the gentle face of Ezra filling my subconscious vision, but the echo of Billy Jennings's voice invading the space of sound.

Billy Jennings showed up to Dolsan's Grocery thirty minutes before the end of my shift. I met his smile with a wave as he stood before the glass of the giant storefront window, making it obvious to the entire sidewalk that he was there waiting for me. Due to the power and influence of one Ms. Elie Jennings, Mr. Dolsan relieved me of my duties early so I could oblige the patient Mr. Billy Jennings.

My mind was with Ezra as I strolled the busy downtown Waynesboro sidewalk with Billy. Waynesboro was a small town, only about two thousand residents or so, so anyone and everyone was very aware of the goings-on of the town's most influential family.

My face scanned the street through a sea of familiar faces, all nodding and smiling, visibly offering their approval of my presence with Billy.

We stopped at Rexman's Drug Store, where Billy bought us both root beer floats. I nervously poked at mine with my straw, while Billy sucked his down like a springtime tornado absorbing the contents of a silo. I couldn't help but admire his handsome beauty as he thoroughly enjoyed his drink. Perhaps, in another time and place, I would fancy the charms and efforts of young Billy, but the reality was, my heart belonged to Ezra, a love I knew the limitations of the law and local society would never allow, much less accept.

"Would ya like to see a picture?" Billy asked, a faint touch of whipped cream dotting the corners of his mouth. "There's the new James Cagney playin' at eight."

I smiled at Billy, wishing I were brave enough to decline his offer. I agreed, though, silently hoping that my prolonged presence with him this evening would fill the quota of his ongoing devotion, at least until he returned to school in a few weeks. As much as I wanted to believe that, I knew it wasn't true.

Billy and I strolled the streets of Waynesboro three times over before he finally found the courage to clasp his hand in mine. His skin was warm and sweaty; my instinct was to swat him away, but I went along with it. My heart fluttered as I thought of Ezra, wondering where he was and what he was thinking. I knew he would be visiting the graveyard, hoping to find me there, but here I was with Billy, holding hands, sipping root beer floats, and now waiting on a picture to start. My disgust and disapproval of myself were nearly palpable.

Billy sat us directly in the center of the theater just as *Blood on the Sun* began to flicker over the silver canvas of Wayne County's sole movie screen. Obviously still confident from the hand holding, Billy wasted no time in placing his arm over my shoulders. His aftershave and cologne battled for dominance over the air around us; his breath seeped a gentle touch of vanilla extract and root beer.

As the picture faded from the screen, Billy turned his face toward me, his lips glistening from the fresh rewetting from his tongue. I stood from my seat, smoothing my skirt with my hands in an assured escape of an impending and unwelcome kiss.

"Would ya like to go to the ridge?" Billy asked once we exited the movie house, nervously kicking a sidewalk pebble. "I could fetch Granny's car and we could head on ova'."

This time, I wasted not a second in declining his offer. I had suffered more than my share of tolerance and patience for the evening.

"No thank ya, Billy. It's time I get back home."

Billy stayed quiet a while, continuing to move the pebble with the tip of his expensive loafer.

"Aw, come on now, Judy. It's been such a fun night. Let's not end it already."

"It has been fun, Billy," I agreed. "But my brotha, Ed, doesn't like it much when I am out past sundown."

"Oh, why worry about ol' Ed?" Billy laughed. "He and I've played pool a few times down at Mamey's bar. He knows I ain't got nothin' but good intentions toward his gorgeous sista."

I flinched as Billy draped his arm over me once more. His insistence did nothing but boil the very last droplets of my patience into evaporated air. I wasn't certain how much longer I could go on being polite.

"Anotha' time, Billy, thank ya."

Billy sighed, obviously annoyed, but agreed.

As we started toward my house, I listened to him beam and brag about life back in Jackson. The way he boasted of his sorority brothers and academic achievements sounded like the spoiled king of some fairy-tale novel detailing the riches of his kingdom. I smiled and nodded when needed, all the while counting the minutes until we would finally arrive at my house.

"Well, Miss Judy Bracewell," Billy announced once we reached the steps of my front porch. My brother and sister had left the front window curtains open, ensuring the light from within would illuminate the entryway. "It was a certain pleasure escortin' ya this evenin'."

I watched in the faint light as Billy Jennings grazed my hand with his lips. Even in the shadows, I saw him lick his lips just before they met my skin, ensuring that his scent and saliva would remain. My stomach grimaced as I viewed a slight string of spit attach itself to his mouth as he retreated his head from my hand.

"I hope ya look forward to my return."

I squinted at him in the darkness, the dim glow of the house behind me darkening my face from his view.

"Sure, Billy," I managed to reply, my throat closing in an attempt to continue to uphold my composure. "I had a nice time tonight, thank ya."

His eyes sparkled in delight as he gave my hand one final wet kiss and turned to walk off into the night.

I waited until he was out of sight before wiping my hand across my skirt. I was nearly to the door, when a familiar voice whispered my name.

I turned to see Ezra standing in the shadows just beyond the light of the front porch. His eyes absorbed the glow from the windows, causing them to gleam and project like two lighthouses on some forgotten shoreline. Immediately, I ran from the porch to greet him.

"Ezra!" I whispered, glancing back over my shoulder to ensure that neither one of my siblings had opened the front door in expectance of me. "What're ya doin' here?"

"I was hopin' to see ya today, Miss Judy-Bee. I don't feel right about the way we left things off last night."

A tear of relief slipped from my right lower lid and down my cheek.

"I was hopin' to see ya too," I whispered, silent as Ezra lifted his hand to wipe my tear as it dazzled its descent in the moonlight.

"Come on," he commanded, gently grasping my wrist and pulling us toward the woods. Moving by memory and moonlight, we reached the old cemetery in record time. Slipping past the broken iron gate, we jumped atop our favorite crypt in unison, as excited and innocent as two schoolchildren boarding a seesaw.

"I'm sorry for the way I acted, Miss Judy-Bee," Ezra spoke into the night, the breath from his mouth billowing white in the spotlight of the lunar orb. "I didn't mean to upset ya."

"No, Ezra," I replied, leaning close to him so I could still whisper. "It's my fault. I'm the one who's sorry. I shoulda neva' forced myself on ya like that. It wasn't polite. It wasn't kind. I'm sorry."

I looked up as Ezra began to chuckle in the darkness.

"Force ya'self? Miss Judy-Bee, ya couldn't force ya'self on me even if ya had an army of ten thousan'."

I shook my head, confused.

"Whaddya mean?"

"I'm sayin'," he answered, moving his face closer to mine, "I've wanted that kiss from the very first moment I eva' laid these ol' Southern boy eyes on ya."

I lost my breath as another tear dripped down my face.

"Oh, Miss Judy-Bee," Ezra cooed, pulling me close to him with both arms. "Please don't cry. How could ya not know that I feel the very same way about ya as ya do me? Always have."

"I know," I whispered into his chest. "I've always known."

A long moment passed before Ezra lifted my face with his fingers.

He moved his gaze over my face, the dazzle of the moon in his eyes bright and effervescent, like two lightning bugs locked inside a pair of mason jars.

"Thing is, Miss Judy-Bee," he spoke, his voice now solemn and firm, "this thing here. This thing we got for each otha'. The way we feel and such . . ."

His eyes lifted into the blackness of the woods. Without looking down, he continued to speak.

"This thing here can get us into a whole world a'trouble."

I shook my head.

"I know, Ezra. But I don't care."

Ezra slowly dropped his eyes back to mine.

"Ya haveta care, Miss Judy," he warned, the moonlight of his eyes fading under the veil of a passing cloud. "I won't stand for ya not carin'."

"But, Ezra—"

"Shh!" he commanded, pressing his index finger over my lips.

The hairs on the back of my neck stood erect as the crunching pop of the nearby ground echoed into the space around us. It was clear that something, or worse yet, someone, was walking this way.

I could feel Ezra's pulse inside his finger as he continued to press it against my lips. I wasn't sure if it was the dampness of the night air or pure terror that caused him to tremble.

After what felt like a lifetime, the footsteps sauntered off, the presence more than likely a passing boar or deer.

"This is what I mean, Miss Judy-Bee," Ezra whispered into my face. "This fear we both livin' here. We can't live our whole lives this way."

I lifted my face to speak, but Ezra stopped me.

"Miss Judy, you gotta let me say my piece."

He placed both hands gently over my cheeks. The light of the moon again dominated the features of his face as the wind moved the shadows of the nearby trees over his skin like spider legs.

"Now, I been doin' nothin' but thinkin' about how I'as gonna say all this to ya," he started, the tremble in his hands returning.

"Ya know I care for ya an awful lot, Miss Judy. And that's why I'm telling ya that we can't sneak around like this no mo'."

My heart fell to the ground as I absorbed his words. A cold drape of loss and rejection cloaked over me in an instant. I started to speak but was interrupted again.

"Miss Judy," Ezra continued, his eyes more dazzled by the arrival of his own tears. "What ya did tonight. Where ya were. Out with that rich boy from town . . ."

He pulled my face closer to his, the warm scent of cinnamon wafting from his tongue as he spoke.

"That's the kinda boy ya need to devote ya time to. Ya need to stop wastin' things away here with me."

"No, Ezra!" I shouted, my voice echoing over the tombstones like the Civil War cannons that had laid many of the young men in the ground beneath us to their final resting place. "Don't tell me to go with a boy like Billy Jennings. That's not what I want!"

"Shh," Ezra said softly, pressing his forehead to mine.

He held me for a long moment before attempting to speak again.

"It's just the way it is, Miss Judy-Bee. There ain't nothin' we can do to change it."

A feeling of rage and disgust flooded over my bones. The unfairness and injustice of the Jim Crow South infuriated me in a way that was difficult to describe. In that moment, I felt that Ezra could read the very thoughts of my mind.

"I know it ain't fair, Miss Judy. Believe me, I know."

I looked up at his face as he continued to hold mine in his hands, careful and sturdy. Though he spoke with such deep passion and emotion, his expression remained calm and stoic.

"Go on with that boy," he directed, wiping another tear from my cheek. "It's just the way it's gotta be."

I didn't have the strength to continue the argument. I simply allowed my head to rest softly against his. Silence drifted into the night sounds, lulling my spinning mind into a root of stillness. I was just about to speak, when the echo of my brother's voice penetrated the distance like faded thunder.

"Ya betta' get goin', Miss Judy-Bee," Ezra spoke tenderly into my hair.

I didn't say a word as he led me from the graveyard and to the edge of the woods just behind my house. Hesitantly, he leaned forward and kissed my forehead gently, pausing for a long moment before removing his lips. Before I could say a word, he was gone, faded into the countless shadows of the dark woods.

It wasn't until my brother's voice again broke the sound of my mind that I found the energy to move. I walked toward the front of the cottage and up the front steps like a zombie from a horror flick I had once seen. If only my brain and emotions could be as empty and vacant as one of those poor creatures'. Instead, my pain overflowed the levee of my conscious mind, spilling the icy water of despair and sorrow over the rest of my being in a unified gush. I stood drowning in my own heartache, when Ed appeared before me.

"Hell, Judith, where the hell have ya been?"

Ed pulled me into the house and secured the broken door before pushing me into the light.

"What's wrong?" he queried, his familiar face and brow scrunched in a look of panic and concern. "Did somethin' happen? Where's Billy? Why ya crying?"

Defeated, I didn't care to muster some form of an alibi or excuse; I simply fell into my big brother's arms, the force of my tears heaving my shoulders and suffocating my breath. Ed pulled me to a chair, lowering me gently into its padded comfort and security.

"Judy," he said softly, his face just inches from mine, "I want ya to tell me what's the matta'. I need ya to be honest."

I shook my head, my tears still too heavy for me to open my eyes.

"Fine," Ed finally agreed. "Let's get ya into bed now. But in the mornin', I'm gonna wanna know what's wrong."

I nodded, the promise of my bed and waiting bout of unconsciousness lifting me from the chair and into Ed's arms.

Francis stirred as Ed guided me into the bed beside her. I kept my eyes closed as he lovingly stroked my hair and cupped my face.

"Get some sleep, Sista," he whispered, careful not to wake Francis. "Whateva' it is, it'll all be okay. I promise."

I nodded my head slightly on the pillow, relieved yet devastated to be home and in my own bed.

The swirling sound of Ezra's voice and words scraped along the sides of my head like steel grating metal. I drifted into the open arms of slumber as broken and defeated as any one girl could ever be.

Thankfully, Ed had to be to work early the next morning, so I was spared his inevitable line of questioning. My assumed freedom was hijacked, however, once my sister, Francis, decided my look of silent despondence was her first order of business.

"What's the matta'?" she questioned, carefully examining my face like a mother cat grooming her kitten. "I can tell somethin's the matta'."

I kept my eyes down as she spoke, lost in my own world of thoughts, which twisted and turned as much as the suction of the sink drain as it swallowed the water I was washing my face with.

I turned away from my sister, intent on making it back to the bed area before she spoke again.

"Hey!" she shouted, clamping her fingers around my forearm. "Now, I don't know much of anything in this world, dear Sista, but I most certainly know when somethin' is the matta' with ya."

Immediately, the tears began to fall, my hurt and upset as obvious and apparent as the spotted array of freckles across my face. I knew any lie or excuse would be energy wasted in futility.

"Go on, now," Francis urged, leading me to the kitchen table. Once she had me seated in a chair, she moved to the kitchen sink to wring out a dishrag. I closed my eyes as she returned with the damp cloth, gently smoothing it over my face with tender care.

"Judith," she stated, pulling my face toward her with the flick of her wrist. "Now, go on. Ya ain't leavin' this house till ya tell me what's the matta'."

I closed my eyes and shook my head, my face still prisoner to her thumb and index finger.

Finally, after what felt like an hour's worth of persuasion, I told my sister everything: the truth about Ezra, my Saturday evenings spent with him and the other boys playing baseball, the hours toiled away in the old cemetery, finally concluding with the heartbreak of the night before.

Francis only looked at me as I spoke, her mouth agape slightly in what I assumed was disbelief. The deafening presence of silence dominated the seconds between us before my sister finally found the words of a response.

"Well . . ." she started, nervously twisting the dishrag in her hands. "Who else knows about this?"

She peered at me from her seat at the kitchen table, her pure blue eyes reflecting the sorrow of my face.

"No one knows," I said faintly. "Only the other boys where we play ball. But they only know that I play with 'em. They don't know how Ezra and I feel about each otha'."

"Yes they do," Francis responded, her face becoming more stern and stone-like. "If ya look at that boy the way ya look when you speak about him, then anyone who is around ya is gonna know."

"That's imposs—"

"Mark my words, Sista. They know."

I watched nervously as her bottom lip intertwined with her teeth. I could tell she was holding back far more than she was saying.

"Don't tell Ed," she finally continued. "It's good that it's ova'. Now just let it be and neva' speak of this to anyone."

I shook my head in sudden disbelief. I couldn't believe or understand why my sister was being so cold and cruel about my feelings or the overall situation. I started to speak, when she interrupted me.

"Don't say anything, Judith," she commanded. "What's done is done. Now, let this be."

"But I love him, Francis."

She glared at me, silent and icy like an Arctic iceberg. I could only breathe as I observed her rise from her chair and inch toward me.

"Now, you listen, dear Sista," she spoke breathlessly. "I ain't gonna stand by and watch some sista of mine go throwin' away her future to the likes of some nigga boy."

Her words stung my ears and scolded my heart as I watched her turn toward the kitchen.

"Ya got the richest boy in Wayne County interested in ya, and all ya can do is sit here and cry over some whim with a colored!"

"Stop!" I shouted, silencing the fury of her voice with just one word.

I turned toward the front door and started to move, when Francis jumped in front of me.

"Ya listen here, Big Sista," she seethed. "Lovin' a nigga ain't gonna get ya nowhere but killed. Where's ya head at? Where's ya sense'a respect?"

I shook my head and pushed for the door.

"Goddammit, Judith!" she screamed, striking my face with an open hand. "Get it togetha'! I won't hear anotha' word about all this."

Holding my throbbing cheek, tears welled beneath my lower lids like the tide invading a dry beachside.

"Don't worry, Sista," I replied strongly and firmly. "Ya won't hear anotha' word from me."

Francis gazed at me for a few seconds before nodding her head in approval.

"Good," she finally remarked. "Good."

Turning toward the front door, I yanked it open with all my remaining strength and fled into the open field that stretched just before the house. I ran until my legs burned; I ran until my heart ached, and I ran until my eyes were so blinded by tears that I could no longer see, crashing into the brush like a wounded animal.

Rolling onto my back, I looked directly at the sun, uncaring as to the enormity of its glow and its effect over the tender flesh of my eyes. I stared for what felt like an eternity, when a shadow suddenly blacked out the light.

"Miss Judy?" I heard Ezra say.

It took several seconds for my eyes to adjust to the scene before me. There, as though from a dream, stood Ezra, strong and handsome above me, almost as if I had conjured him through the falling of my tears.

"Are you okay?"

He knelt before me, swatting insects from my face and brushing rogue hairs from their matted placement over my eyes.

Silently, I shook my head, feeling him lean into the brush and pull me toward him.

"Come on," he said comfortingly, "let's get ya back to ya house."

I didn't resist as we walked the distance of the field. So much of what I had considered a certainty in my life had popped and faded like a rainbow-colored bathtub bubble. Ezra, my sister: it was all too much to bear. Before I knew it, we were bounding up the stairs of the front porch, Ezra stopping just short of the front door before turning me to face him.

"It's gonna be okay, Miss Judy-Bee," he whispered toward my ear. "Everything is gonna be just fine. You'll see."

Francis appeared in the window, her face glaring through the blurred thickness of the glass.

I watched Ezra's eyes widen with fear as he caught sight of her, gripping my hand in his.

"Ya take care now, Miss Judy-Bee," he said gently. "Don't be so hard on ya'self."

He turned his head back toward the now empty window.

"Or ya sista. Don't be so hard on her eitha'. She loves ya."

He started to descend the front porch steps, when the sound of the always-stuck front door thundered open.

"Ya go on now, nigga. Get ya ass off this porch!"

Francis's words were rivaled only by that of her angry face. I stood in disbelief as I watched my sister shoo at Ezra the way a farmer goes after a coyote sniffing near his chicken coop.

I looked to Ezra, who dropped his head to his chest before turning and making his way around the side of the house.

"And don't let me catch ya back around here again!" she hollered. "Not only will I call Sheriff, but I also know how to use a shotgun!"

"Enough!" I screamed, my voice so loud and sudden that the inner lining of my throat screeched and cracked as though I had just swallowed a can of acid.

A fury like I had never known in my sister raged behind her eyes.

"Get inside," she hissed, pointing to the open door of the house. "I ain't done dealin' with ya."

Wiping my face with my arm, I inched toward my sister.

"Ya ain't Momma," I seethed. "There ain't shit left for ya to say."

"Oh yes there is, little miss!" she screamed, spinning on her heels to grab at my hair. "Do ya understand the shame and horror ya could bring to this family by allowin' this nigga to be around ya?"

Turning to face her, I pulled my hair from her grasp and stood straight.

"Ya've said all that ya need to, Francis. There ain't nothin' left here for us to discuss."

Disappearing into the house, I tucked behind the bedroom curtain and began to dress for work. Francis didn't say another word until I was walking out the front door.

"As I said," she spoke angrily, "ya betta' neva' speak a word'a this to Ed."

I slammed the door shut behind me, following the pull of my eager feet as they ventured toward town. With my head spinning, my temples aching, and my face burning, I threw open the door to Dolsan's Grocery just in time to hear Billy Jennings shout my name.

Pretending I didn't hear him, I headed toward the broom closet to fetch my apron. A second or two later, I heard the store's door chime signal Billy's arrival.

"Hey, Judy!" he called. "I was yellin' for ya from the street."

His face dropped once he ventured his eyes over my face.

"What's the matta', Judy. Ya okay?"

I nodded, pursed my lips, and moved toward the deli counter.

"Hey," he said softly, stopping my movement with his body. "Talk to me, Judy."

I lifted my face in cold defiance.

"Billy," I started, the wealth of pain and upset within me swelling to the surface of my throat in a calm and easy stream, "please stop comin' around here."

His brow twisted in confusion. I felt him back off slightly.

"I have no interest in ya, Billy Jennings. I'm tired of actin' kind and polite toward ya. Ya a nice enough young man, but honestly, Billy, I just don't feel the same way about ya as ya do me."

Billy's expression completely morphed, almost as if he had put on some kind of mask. I couldn't tell if he was hurt, shocked, or about to explode.

"Now, I'd appreciate it if ya'd just go on home to your granny's and just leave me be for the rest of the time ya visitin' here."

Stepping around Billy, I slipped behind the counter and began to shuffle some wax paper. I didn't look, but I could feel him staring at me.

Without a word or so much as a sound, Billy turned toward the front of the store and sauntered out to the sidewalk. I looked up just in time to see him turn back a moment, glance at me, and then return to the movement of his legs.

I hardly spoke a word to anyone for the entirety of my shift. Mr. Dolsan could sense that something was the matter; I could tell by the way he kept staring at me from time to time. Still, he never said a word, perhaps wise to the wrath of disturbing a voluntarily silent female.

Had I known what was to take place that night after I left Dolsan's Grocery, perhaps I would have never left at all.

2

Ain't No Justice for a Black Man

The buzzing cicadas sirened their warning over the blackened red dirt road that carried me home. With the sun long set, no moon nor stars illuminated my path. Instead, an endless stream of fast-moving, billowing clouds suffocated the sky, their ominous rumbling signaling the approach of a storm.

I jumped as a flash of lightning charged over the treetops and into the sightless yonder. The clap of thunder that quickly followed alerted all that lay below its echo of the dangerous closeness of the power of electricity. The sudden thunder quickened my pulse and hastened my pace. I felt large drops of cold, wet rain begin to assault my skin as I followed my feet from a light skip to a run. I was nearly to the first fork in the road, when another flash of lightning thundered overhead, causing me to trip over my own shoes and land face-first into the now rain-covered clay road.

Cursing under my breath, I resurrected my stance, brushing the mud off my slacks as best I could. I attempted to regain my brisk movement, when the distinct sound of the snapping of nearby tree branches stunned my senses. The thudded plop of footsteps trudging through the fresh mud sent a chilled shiver down my spine, screaming for my feet to lift and bolt for safety. But before I could move an inch, the blunt force of a far larger human knocked me from my feet and off the side of the clay road. I opened my mouth to cry out, but a fistful of red dirt was shoved over my tongue and into my throat. I felt myself being dragged into the nearby brush, the darkness of the world around me completely concealing my attacker.

I started to squirm and attempt an escape from the mystery assailant's grasp, when I was lifted into the air, turned over onto my belly, and tossed violently to the earth below. My face pounded into something hard as my body dropped onto the foliage-covered floor of the forest. I could feel the mud inside my mouth slide deeper into my throat as my face was forcefully pressed further into the earth. My ears could only distinguish the wicked rhythm of the pouring rain and accented thunderclaps as my belt was removed and my slacks lowered. I summoned my legs to kick, but quickly realized that the mystery presence was forcing its weight over the entirety of my lower body. The collected years of virtue and innocence ran from my being atop the countless streams of rainwater that snaked out around me. My awareness began to flicker and fade as the force of the stranger's appendage tore into the crevasses of my intimate female flesh without caution or concern. Just as the darkness of the ground against my face began to give way to the blackness of unconsciousness, I heard the voice of Ezra echo over the soaked pine needles and dry leaves that shrouded the space around me. In that moment, the weighted presence of the intruder was removed from my back and pulled into the slight distance behind me. The warbled sound of two male voices tumbled and blurred into the hollow column of awareness that slowly slipped from my cognitive control and into the abyss of the unconscious.

A final blast of lighting fizzled overhead, its strike and movement close enough to erect the light hairs of my arms and behind my neck.

The instant follow of cracking thunder eased my mind as I slipped beyond the final slope of consciousness and into the silent unknown.

"Ya know I've always loved ya, Miss Judy-Bee."

The faint sensation of lips pressed against my forehead pulled me from the darkness and into the dim glow of a strange room. The retreating shadow of someone leaving the area could be seen just as I opened my eyes.

Terrified, I took in the scene around me: a sterile white room, a small bedside table, a softly lit lamp, a stainless-steel pole holding a clear bag of liquid.

The fog of my brain started to lift as I recognized that I was in a hospital. I looked down at my body, which was tightly secured beneath the immaculate press of firmly tucked snow-white bedsheets. A small fan buzzed in the corner, providing a faint breeze that tickled my face and flicked at my hair.

Then, the flood of memory began to surge through my awareness. The attack in the woods. It all came back to me: the cold rain, the presence of the stranger, the force of his body against my own. A tear fell from my left eye as I relived the horror, the cool waft of the fan quickly drying it away.

There was another bed next to mine, but it was empty. I could sense more lighting beyond the door of the room, but I heard no movement, no voices. I assumed I was in Wayne County Hospital. I started to wonder about Ed and Francis. Did they know I was here? Were they aware of what had happened to me?

I recalled hearing Ezra's voice during the attack. Was he the one who had brought me here?

Thoughts and images of the nightmare reality taunted and swirled within my head as vivid and detailed as if they were occurring all over again. It was only when my sobbing subsided that I relaxed enough to fall into a deep sleep.

"Oh, my dear sista."

I opened my eyes to see Francis, her crimson-red lips smiling at me softly, her eyes dazzling with tears.

"I could barely sleep a wink last night," she continued, adjusting her position in the bedside chair. "I woulda stayed here with ya had they allowed me to. I didn't wanna leave once I saw ya."

I watched in silence as tears began to flood down the blush-painted cheeks of my only sister. An odd feeling washed over me as I witnessed her emotion. Despite the fact I had only just woken from a restful, powerful sleep, the overwhelming sense that something wasn't quite as it seemed seeped over my core, coldly and firmly.

I allowed my eyes to tour the room. Countless beams of sunshine penetrated through the blinds that covered the windows like bullet holes through a highway sign. The details of the various medical machinery and equipment could now be seen in the shadow-less spotlight of the various sun rays.

I returned my eyes to Francis, who now focused all her attention on a small compact mirror, busily reapplying her face powder.

I waited for her attention to return to me before I spoke, a moment of stillness that lasted far longer than it should have.

"How did I get here?" I questioned, watching her dab the remaining moisture from her eyes with a crumpled tissue.

"Ya don't know?" Francis questioned, almost coyly.

I waited for a moment before shaking my head.

"No, Francis. I don't know."

A slight smile settled on Francis's lips as she started to speak. The way she straightened her back and fluttered her lashes, it was almost as if her answer had been meticulously planned and rehearsed.

I watched in wonder as my sister dramatically detailed the account of my fate after I had lost consciousness.

"Ya owe ya very life to Billy Jennings," she replied, almost excitedly. "He saved ya last night."

I felt my brow furrow in confusion.

"Yes!" Francis exclaimed, noticing my shock. "He was makin' his way out to our house, when he heard some sorta commotion in the bushes. Come to find out, it was that damn nigga boy havin' his way with ya. You was out cold, so ya won't rememba'."

I darted my eyes over my sister's face, the enormity of her words washing over me in a convulsion of tears. I struggled to catch my breath between long pauses of uncontrolled sobbing.

"Oh, Sista," Francis cooed, inching toward me for an embrace. I forcefully pushed her back.

"No!" I shot at her with clear and sturdy words. "What ya sayin' didn't occur. Ya lyin', Francis. It's a lie!"

I could see my frantic expression in the glimmering gaze of Francis's stark blue eyes. That same coy-like smile took its place over her lipstick-heavy lips as she readied her reply.

"How would ya know, dear Sista? You was unconscious. You was attacked. Billy saved ya from surely being killed by that black animal."

I shook my head, tears whipping from my skin like a summer sprinkler.

"I was awake, Francis. I heard Ezra. He must'a pulled whoever it was off'a me. Billy Jennings had nothin' to do with it."

My heart froze as the final words of my sentence rolled from my tongue. The chilling realization that it very well could have been Billy Jennings who attacked me in the woods pierced at every fragile corner of my soul. My heart began to race as the sightless picture became clearer. I forced myself up in the bed, tugging at the blankets in an attempt to escape my confinement.

"Judy!" Francis snapped. "Lie back in that bed. Don't ya even think of movin' from there."

"It's a lie, Francis! Someone is lyin'! Billy is lyin'! Ezra would never do somethin' like that to me. Neva'! To me, or to anyone."

My breathing rivaled the rampant pace of my heart as I took in Francis's response. An icy tinge of fear oozed over my skin as horrid and rancid as a pus-filled boil bursting from the backside of a wild boar.

"Ya such a fool, dear Sista," Francis replied without emotion. "Ya just too damn innocent to realize that all Negro men will rape a white woman as soon as they are given the chance. I done told ya how dangerous it was to be seen around him. Ya brought this upon ya'self. All I'm sayin' is ya betta' be thankin' the Good Lord above that Billy Jennings happened to pass by to save ya dumb nigga-lovin' ass."

I couldn't speak. All words betrayed me as I absorbed the power and venom of my sister's certain statement. I didn't know what to believe, but I knew in the depths of all that was true and justified that Ezra would never lay a finger on me.

"Where's Billy now?" I asked, the panic and terror of my expression still beaming back at me in the tear-glittered gaze of Francis's eyes. I now wasn't sure if her tears were those of sorrow, or those of joy.

"He rode with us to the hospital last night, but headed back to his granny's once they got ya settled. Ed went and got the Benson boys . . . they went out to find the nigga."

My heart nearly jolted from my chest as I soaked in the reality of her reply. Again, I tried to escape the bed.

"Ya listen here, Sista," Francis hissed into my face, her skin so close to mine that I could smell the density of her face powder. "Ya let justice be done, ya hear?"

Tears flooded my face as I sat motionless between the stack of hospital pillows and the firm, angry grip of my sister's arm.

"Things will be taken care of."

"No!" I shouted, pushing my sister from before me, stumbling slightly as I hobbled toward the doorway. "I don't care who said what. I'm tellin' ya now that Ezra did not do this!"

Francis's smirk melted and morphed into a jovial grin, the sound of her familiar voice fading into a foreign, sinister chuckle.

"Oh, Sista," she started, rising from her seat and inching toward me. "Even if what ya believe is true, it won't matta' anyways. Not only is Billy Jennings a white man, but he is the son of the attorney general, not to mention the grandson of the town's most respected, revered, and distinguished citizen. Do ya really think anyone is gonna believe some po'-ass Negro boy over someone as beloved and cherished as Billy?"

The harsh reality of her statement snaked around my being like the jaws of a hungry rattler consuming its prey. I nearly fainted from the weakness brought on by sudden defeat. Just as I began to step back toward my sister, the room started to spin; Francis's height towered over me as I fell to the cold linoleum floor below. The same taciturn smirk plastered on Francis's face as I turned over onto my back, her satisfied eyes peering down at me as I faded into the dizzying spin behind my lids.

I awoke to the sight of my brother, Ed, and what I presumed to be a doctor, in a white lab coat, standing near the doorway of my hospital room. I couldn't hear what they were saying, and it wasn't until I began to move and fidget around in the bed, that they turned their heads in my direction.

"Hey, baby girl!" Ed beamed as he quickly darted to the bed-side. "I'm so happy to see those beautiful eyes!"

The feeling of my brother's strong, muscular arms draping around my shoulders sent a warm rush of safety and comfort through-out my veins. It was as if the blood of my core had recognized its own identity within the inner circulation of my kin.

Neither of us spoke for a long while as I held on to him, firm and steady. A flow of silent tears marched down my face as I settled into the stark contrast of my brother's comforting presence versus that of my sister's cold and intimidating stare. My eyes scoured the room over Ed's shoulder in search of Francis, but thankfully, she was nowhere to be seen.

"Doc says ya ready to get outta here now," Ed smiled at me, his warm eyes and tobacco-sweet breath cooling over the tracks of my tears.

"He said ya had quite a spill earlia' . . . tryin' to get up and walk around the room and such."

I continued to hold onto Ed, uncaring and unable to fill him in on the earlier encounter with our sister.

"He said they had ya loaded up with all sorts of medicine and tranquiliza's. He's surprised as hell that ya was able to move at all, much less get up and venture 'round the room."

"Oh, Ed," I whispered into his worn work shirt. "Please, just take me home."

Ed and I enjoyed the silence as we journeyed the familiar dirt road that led from town to our house. The tension within the cab of his beat-up, old Dodge Plymouth pickup became dense and heavy as we neared the site of my attack.

I looked at Ed's face as the area skirted past us and out of sight. Ed's knuckles were tight and ghost white as he firmly gripped the steering wheel.

Surprised at my own lack of emotion, I took one last glance out the back window of the pickup at the place of my real-life horror, and then back to the face of my beloved brother.

I kept my eyes steady over his as I formed the words to my burning question.

"Where's Ezra?" I asked, my eyes still and unblinking. "I know ya went afta' him. Please, Ed, tell me where he is."

A shadow fell over my brother's face; a look I had never seen on him before cloaked his entire body the moment my words dropped from my lips.

"Ed," I prompted, his silence shaking the certainty of my voice.

"It's handled," he answered dryly, his earlier warmth and comfort fading from his energy as quick as a winter cold front.

"Whaddya mean, 'It's handled'? What did you boys do to him?"

Ed snapped his head in my direction, his eyes wide and dripping with heavy tears.

"Whaddya mean, 'What did we do to him'?" he slurred, his falling tears overcoming his composure. "That boy raped ya and ya here askin' what we did to him?"

to speak just as he slammed on the truck's rickety and groaning brakes.

"The question you should be asking ya'self, Sista, is what did he do to you?"

Ed's eyes beamed across the short distance between us, their wide and watery gaze appearing to have a life of their own.

"He raped ya, Judy," he stated, coldly and hauntingly. "That boy deserves whateva' it was that happened to him."

Despite the discomfort of the moment, I refused to turn away. I refused to allow this conversation to end without knowing exactly what it was these boys did to my Ezra.

"Where is he, Ed?" I asked again, this time, the inner strength of every ounce of oxygen within my lungs forcing my emotionless composure.

Ed remained silent for a long while before shaking his head. "It's been handled."

Regardless of my pleading, Ed refused to disclose any further information regarding Ezra. He barreled the truck toward our house and declined to speak to me even once we arrived there. I spent the next three hours interrogating my brother, only to receive a silent yet somehow sympathetic silence.

Even when I punched and screamed at him, he remained silent, the tears in his eyes never fading from the shelter of his lower lids.

It was only when Francis arrived home that I discontinued my questioning. Instead of joining my siblings for dinner, I marched behind the bedroom curtain and allowed myself the surrender of another spell of undisrupted slumber.

The sun was clearly visible through the windows of the cottage when I finally came to. A soft yet rapid knocking on the front door jolted me from my peace.

I slowly lifted myself from the bed, the sound of my sister opening the door filling the space of the living area.

"Is Judy here, ma'am?" I heard a familiar voice ask. My heart stopped in my chest as I raced to the door.

"Ezra!" I screamed, a burst of tears instantaneously combusting from my sleep-weary eyes. I pulled the doorknob from Francis's grasp, forcing the front door open further until it hit the wall beside it.

"No ma'am," Ezra's brother, Jordan, said, his eyes locking with mine. "I'as wonderin' if ya'd seen Ezra though. We ain't seen him since yesterday evenin', and the family's gettin' worried. My momma's about to lose her mind. It ain't like Ezra to just up and disappear this way."

My heart sank as my brain recounted the horrific circumstances of my reality. I could feel Francis burning to take over the situation.

"Sorry, boy," she said in a semi-hiss, fetching the door from the wall. "We ain't seen him."

She started to close the door completely, when I interjected.

"Wait! Jordan . . ."

I felt the sizzle of my sister's glare as I passed her and moved onto the front porch.

Without so much as even glancing back at her, I pulled Jordan's hand in mine and led him toward the side of the house.

I never heard the front door close, so I knew Francis was still standing guard, despite being out of sight.

"Jordan," I whispered, the urgency of my words pulling more tears down my face, "ya need to contact Sheriff. I really believe somethin' terrible has happened to ya brotha. Please, go to Sheriff and tell him ya think Ezra's been kidnapped."

Jordan shifted his unblinking gaze over mine, the soul behind his eyes embracing my fear and panic.

"Billy Jennings and the Benson boys think Ezra attacked me in the woods last night. It ain't true, a'course; I know Ezra would neva' do such a thing. Still, the very fact that they're sayin' he did puts him in grave danga'."

Jordan's eyes froze over; an unfamiliar look I had yet to witness on the face of any human being slowly began to unfurrow down his expression like an old and heavy stage curtain closing out an encore.

"Ya need to go now, Jordan," I urged, pulling his hand closer to my chest as I breathlessly delivered my plea.

"I'm sorry, Miss Judy," Jordan spoke, his voice and inflection reminiscent of his brother's. "I can't just go to Sheriff that way."

Jordan stepped back, slowly releasing his hand from my trembling grasp.

"Thank ya for tellin' me though, Miss Judy."

I watched in complete disbelief as the young boy turned and began to trudge into the woods behind the house.

"Wait!" I cried, stumbling toward him over the broken stems of various shrubs and overgrown weeds. "I'll go with ya."

Jordan gaped at me for several seconds, a look of pity and defeat now frozen over his boyish face.

"That's alright, Miss Judy," he responded, his eyes glazed as he forced a polite smile. "I appreciate ya offerin'. I know you and my brotha is real good friends."

"No, Jordan," I sobbed, the weight of my emotion forcing me to my knees. "We haveta find him. We haveta make sure he's okay. We need Sheriff to help us."

Jordan peered down at me, his face twisting in a myriad of emotion. Finally, after what felt like hours, he spoke, offering me his hand in order to assist me to my feet.

"Ya don't understan', Miss Judy," he started, his voice solemn and stone as if spoken with a voice three times his years. "If those boys goin' aroun' sayin' my brotha did what ya said . . . there ain't no use involvin' Sheriff, ma'am."

"But he didn't do it!" I shouted, turning my head toward the house just in time to see Francis lift the bedroom curtain. "Someone attacked me, but it wasn't him. I know it wasn't him. It couldn't a'been. I believe he saved me though. He was there, but he most certainly did not lay a finga' a'harm on me. I just know he didn't. I promise the world he didn't. I swear to all that is holy he didn't!"

Jordan's eyes reflected mine; the same look of terror and uncertainty that gripped my expression now cloaked his face.

"It won't matta', Miss Judy," Jordan whispered, he too spotting Francis in the not-so-distant window. "The fact of 'em sayin' it makes him guilty. There ain't no justice for a black man."

I watched Jordan disappear into the brush that led into the deeper part of the woods. Within seconds, he was gone, and I was left with only the painful echo of his words to guide my steps back to the front of the house.

The terrifying reality of Jordan's statement solidified around my racing heart, tight and unrelenting. Jordan was right. There was no justice for a black man.

3

Help Me Find Ezra

I spent the next three days in bed. I refused to speak to my sister, and Ed refused to speak to me. Both Ed and Francis ate their dinner meals separately, whereas I ate mine alone in bed. While the sun continued its usual journey over the sky and my siblings went about their daily lives, my entire being remained transfixed by the unfathomable weight of my worry for Ezra. I hardly slept, and when I did manage to surrender to unconsciousness, the fate of my beloved Ezra haunted my dreams. Nightmares of him hungry and terrified, hiding out in some remote location in the woods, or tied up and captive, held prisoner by the Benson boys. Even my subconscious refused to entertain any thought or vision of Ezra's possible demise; the very mention of the subject across the forefront of my mind was immediately overwhelmed and disintegrated by the power and strength of my burning hope and faith. I simply had to believe that Ezra was still alive. I had to. To not was to give up on my own will and desire to live.

On the evening of the fourth day, Billy Jennings arrived, his unannounced presence the only change in my current existence to inspire me to venture from the bed and change into something other than my decade-old nightgown. Francis was out in town, while Ed was still working, so Billy and I had the cottage to ourselves. I wasted no time in interrogating him for any drop or shred of detail or information he might know.

Billy insisted that after he had returned home to his granny's house on the night of the attack, he never heard another word about Ezra. In what I assumed was an attempt distract me, he aimed the focus of the conversation toward my mental, emotional, and physical recovery, promising to assist in whatever way he could.

"What happened to ya, Judy . . ." Billy whispered, slight tears meandering on the edges of both of his eyes, "it just breaks my heart."

"I need to know what happened, Billy," I fired back, my patience unamused with his sudden display of emotion. "Please, Billy. I need for ya to tell me anything ya may know."

Billy looked down at the worn-out floorboards of the front porch for what felt like an eternity before lifting his eyes back to mine.

"I don't know nothin', Judy. I swear. All I know is I found ya in a very bad way that night. May God show no mercy on that boy for doin' what he did to you."

I listened to Billy babble on about unrelated and unimportant details of self-centered abandon for another few minutes before dismissing him completely. The frozen image of Billy's shocked and irritated face as I slammed the front door on him lingered in my mind as I returned to bed. I must have fallen asleep because I didn't recall another thought or conscious vision until Francis crawled into the bed beside me, the sun now vacated from beyond the white lace curtain of the tiny bedroom window.

"Why will no one tell me the truth?" I whispered at Francis, the distance between us only a mere inch or so atop the small mattress.

"I just wanna know what happened to him."

I could see Francis's eyes flickering beneath her large lids before she returned a reply. I could tell she was resistant to any form of conversation or mention of this topic. Still, I was prepared to persist for however long necessary. I wasn't about to allow my sister to escape into the responsibility-free arms of slumber without receiving some form of acknowledgment to my question.

"Let it go, Sista," she finally replied in a whisper far lower than my own, obviously conscious not to disturb Ed, who was snoring loudly just beyond the curtain that separated my sister's and my sleeping area from his.

"No!" I shouted back, purposing releasing my voice to a tone far higher than a whisper.

"Shh!" Francis hissed, quickly cupping her hand over my mouth. "Ya need to let this go, Sista. I beg of ya, just let it go."

I shook my head, pulling my face from beneath the press of her hand.

"I won't, Francis. It ain't fair. I need to know what happened to him."

"What ya need to know is that ya alive after a crazed, horny colored boy attacked you in the woods!"

Francis's eyes appeared to glow in the darkness, the fury of her words creating an invisible fire between us. "I done told ya that ya should be thankin' God for allowin' Billy to save ya that night."

I waited for her breathing to subside from the obvious pressure of her angered emotion before continuing.

"I don't believe that's what happened," I spoke plainly, forcing my words at her ear in a hopeful attempt at releasing some truth from her.

"Ezra loved me, Francis. The same way I loved him. We're in love. He'd never hurt me."

"Shut up!" Francis seethed, rising from the bed and slamming her weight over my body.

With my sister now directly on top of me, my limbs were useless under the forceful press of her entire being. I could smell the Colgate on her breath as she spat her heated words over my face.

"Ya listen now and ya listen good," she snarled. "I don't care whatcha think ya felt about that nigga boy. The truth is, it don't matta' anyways. Ya know damn good and well a nigga and a white woman ain't never gonna be allowed. Why go on foolin' ya'self of anything different?"

I felt her roll herself back onto her side of the bed, her breathing again rapid and fired.

"Just let it be, Judith," she warned, attempting to slow her breathing to the cadence of her whisper. "I just thank the Good Lord ya alive and here to move on from this. I just wish ya'd do the same."

I decided it best just to leave the conversation be as it was. There was no sense in pressing Francis any further. If anything, I was only shutting her down more, the chances of her ever revealing to me any detail she knew becoming less and less with every rise and fall of her anger-battered chest.

Silently, I cried myself to sleep, the feeling of abandon and hopelessness shrouding my flesh in a painful yet somehow warm sensation. I surrendered to its grip, too drained and too exhausted to resist.

Finally, after two long weeks trapped in a self-imprisonment of bedridden despair and depression, I forced myself to return to work. Mr. Dolsan never mentioned a word to me regarding my absence, much less the reason for it. I caught him staring at me curiously throughout the shift, the worrisome look on his face that of a concerned parent or guardian. I opted not to confront him on it, his apparent concern for me somehow filling the void of parental involvement I so clearly missed and lacked in my life.

I was just hanging my apron in the broom closet, when a strange young man I had never seen before, decked from head to toe in his Sunday best, stood before me, a look of nervous curiosity draped over his expression.

"Excuse me, miss," he stumbled, his words broken by a clear crack in his voice. "Are you Ms. Judith Bracewell?"

My heart flinched after he delivered my name. A sudden pang of fear and uncertainty began to snake through my veins. I darted my eyes around the store nervously, somehow fearful that this unexpected interaction would attract the attention of curious onlookers, or worse yet, Mr. Dolsan. After seeing no other soul besides the overdressed man before me, I returned my eyes to his, my reflection wobbling back at me in the nervous gaze of the stranger.

"Yes," I whispered, clearly indicating to him that I didn't want our conversation to be overheard.

Following my lead, the young man darted his eyes around him, quickly turning his head in both directions before speaking.

"Would you mind if I had a quick word with you?"

Hesitantly, I agreed, nodding for him to follow me out of the store. Once secluded on the street corner, just about a block or so from Dolsan's, I turned to face the young man again.

"Who are ya?" I asked, my eyes continuing to dart nervously over the street.

"Sorry, Ms. Bracewell," the young man replied, nodding his head and offering his hand. "I'm Luke Pinder, Tenth Circuit Court assistant district attorney."

I looked at his hand cautiously before placing my own hand over it. The cold clamminess of the man's flesh slid and suctioned my skin to his like a slug on a tree branch. Quickly, I pulled my hand back to my side.

"The DA's office has been informed about the mysterious disappearance of a young Negro male."

The young man narrowed his eyes over mine, a faint glimmer of excitement charging over his expression.

"My sources have told me to speak with you for more information."

My eyes widened, my heart accelerating its patter. I felt the world begin to spin around me. It wasn't until I made the conscious effort to acknowledge and control my breathing, that I was able to muster a reply.

"I . . ." I fumbled, my words as heavy and uncertain as the young man's earlier introduction. "I . . ."

"I understand," the man spoke softly. "Would it be better if we found some other place to talk?"

I followed his eyes over the distance of Main Street, various sprinklings of residents covering the sidewalk and street crossings like ants on a dirt mound.

"Um . . ." I swallowed hard, the sound of my own saliva deafening to my ears.

"Would you mind if I escorted you home?"

I moved my eyes over his, completely uncertain as to what to do, yet somehow confident that I could trust him.

After a few more warbled attempts at speaking, I finally agreed to allow Mr. Pinder to walk with me toward home. I listened beneath the relentless echo of my own heartbeat and breathing as he detailed the reason for his visit.

"Due to my background as a civil rights attorney, the DA hired me just after the two white men who were acquitted in the murder of a young Negro boy over in Leflore County back in '55 sold their story to a magazine, openly admitting their guilt. That's double jeopardy for you. Just prior to that, I worked for a firm in Massachusetts that specializes in civil rights cases. We assisted the NAACP in several high-profile trials. I figured I could be of more service practicing in a state that enforces Jim Crow laws, so I packed up and moved to Mississippi. I was admitted to the state bar and hired by the Tenth Circuit Court district attorney all within a year."

I looked up at him, unsure as to what to say in response. Luke noticed and continued to pepper the silence with comforting words regarding progress and justice. I had to admit, the sound and meaning of his words resonated within me in some deep, hidden place I had yet to fully understand or experience. I lost all sense of time and presence as I fell headfirst into the extraordinary depth of his words.

"Do you know where Ezra Washington is?"

Hearing Mr. Pinder refer to Ezra's full name nearly stopped my heart. It was clear that whoever had contacted him was keenly aware of the interpersonal details of the situation. Though my mind continued to frazzle and spin in a whirling rotation of uncertainty and confusion, that inner voice deep below my breastbone again confirmed that I could trust him.

"I don't know," I managed to whisper, my voice sunken and hollow. "I wish ta God I did though."

I looked over at Luke, my vision blinded by the clouding of tears.

"Stop," I heard Luke say, gently placing his hands over my shoulders. "What exactly happened here, Ms. Bracewell?"

"Judy . . ." I whispered. "Please, just call me Judy."

I spent the next ten minutes attempting to detail the past couple of weeks under the weighted force of sobbing convulsions. I didn't resist when Luke finally pulled me to his chest for a firm and lingering embrace. He didn't say a word as I attempted to recount the mysterious and unsolved circumstances that surrounded the attack. He didn't even furrow a brow when I confirmed to him that I didn't believe it was Ezra who was responsible.

Luke Pinder continued to question me, scribbling down various keywords and phrases into a small notebook as we slowly made our way toward my house. My tears began to dry and my breathing soften as I became used to the sound and presence of Luke's voice. I couldn't help but notice how handsome he was with his baby-blue eyes piercing out from under the shadow of his carefully combed sandy-blond hair. His smile was infectious, the way he nervously cleared his throat before starting a new sentence both comforting and endearing. I felt myself completely absorb into his voice and smile, fully unobservant or aware when the unmistakable throttle of Ed's work truck settled beside us.

"What's goin' on, Judy?" I heard my brother ask, his unexpected voice interrupting Luke's and my conversation like a sewing needle pricking the flesh of a party balloon.

"Hey, Ed." I smiled, turning my head in his direction.

Ed stared at me, his eyes darting over my face and back to Luke's. I could see Luke's entire body in the reflection of Ed's large brown eyes as he scanned over the stranger's complete presence, cautiously and curiously.

"Hi, sir," Luke finally spoke, stepping toward Ed's truck and offering his hand. "I'm Tenth Circuit Court assistant district attorney Luke Pinder. Nice to meet you."

Ed just looked at Luke's hand for a long moment. When he finally lifted his eyes, the presence of severe caution and distrust blanketed his entire visible body.

"Get in the truck, Judy," he commanded, keeping his eyes firmly fixed over Luke's.

"But, Ed. I—"

"Now!" he hollered, the piercing tone of his voice reminiscent of our late father's.

I smiled briefly at Luke, who returned the smile with a friendly nod, and made my way to the passenger side of Ed's truck.

I was barely in the cab, when Ed punched the accelerator, the back tires of the Dodge Plymouth disturbing the mud, dirt, and gravel of the clay road into a frenzied, billowing cloud of debris that soaked over Luke like a swarm of locusts. Peering through the dust-plastered back window of the truck, I could see a muck-covered Luke wiping his face as he feverishly attempted to escape the assault of the dirt cloud. Ed didn't speak a word to me until we were parked in front of the house.

"Ya stay away from that man, ya hear?" he said in a stern and firm voice, his hands cupped over mine. "That boy is just here tryin' ta stir up some trouble, and we best not do or say anything to give it to him."

"But, Ed, he said—"

"No!" Ed shouted, his eyes wider and more terrified than I had ever seen them before. "Not anotha' word to him, Judy. Do ya understand me?"

I stared at my brother with a frozen expression, my heart accelerating under the foreign scowl of his face.

"Do ya?" he shook me, his calloused hands tightening over mine.

"Yes!" I cried, both from the physical pain of his grip and the emotional enormity of the entire ordeal. "I understand, Ed."

Ed just looked at me for few seconds before pulling me closer to him. I could sense his fear and anger fading to the heaviness of his concern for me.

"I know ya been through hell the last few weeks, Sis," he whispered into my hair, the smell of his breath sweet from the aroma of chewing tobacco and beer. "I just don't think ya fully understand what kinda' trouble can come of all this if we ain't careful."

I didn't respond. I didn't know how to. My mind was still lost and heavy from the promise and substance of the conversation I'd had with Luke. So much of what he had said had resonated deep within me in that place I was now conscious of, and both excited and now curious to explore.

It wasn't until Francis appeared on the front porch, that Ed and I finally exited the truck and made our way into the house. I didn't speak another word to either of my siblings for the rest of the night. I finished off my supper, assisted Francis with the cleanup, and wrapped myself beneath the covers of the bed, the unspoken promise of information and possible justice adding to the fear-ridden blandness of my dreams.

"Nice to see you again, Judy."

I looked up from the deli counter to see Luke Pinder, his handsome face beaming a friendly and welcoming smile, his hair still neatly combed, and his suit a different style and shade of brown than the one he had worn the day before.

"I'm sorry about yesterday," he continued, his smile softening to a look of worry and concern. "I didn't mean to cause any upset between you and your brother."

"It's all right," I started, a nervous shade of blush pinkening my face. "I just—wait, how'd ya know that was my brotha?"

Luke's eyes smiled, though his face reflected a nervous haze of caution and concern.

"I've done my research, Judy," he finally replied, straightening his powder-blue tie with both hands. "I was given the names of several points of interest. I always make sure to figure out who everyone is before making my approach."

Ed's words of warning echoed around me as though he were here repeating them. Nervously, I lowered my attention back to the clumped morsels of lunchmeat that dotted the small counter.

"I see. Well, Mr. Pinder, it was certainly very nice to spend that walk with ya yesterday, but I'm afraid I'm gonna haveta ask ya to leave me alone from now on. My brotha, as ya mentioned, is most certainly not too keen on me speakin' with ya."

I could feel Luke's eyes on me, his thoughts and worry nearly audible from inside his fast-moving brain.

"Well, I do apologize again," he stated, nervously clearing his throat before continuing. "Still, I'm afraid I'll need some more information from you so I can proceed with my investigation."

I looked up at him, a sudden fear gripping my throat.

"What investigation, Mr. Pinder? No one here has committed a crime."

"I understand, Judy, but until Ezra Washington has been located, safe and secure, his disappearance has the interest of the governor, the firm I used to work for in Massachusetts, and not to mention the NAACP."

Despite my endless and relentless worry and longing for Ezra, I couldn't help but feel that Luke was somehow homing his suspicions in on Ed. Without interference, my sisterly instinct to protect Ed centered itself on the forefront of my awareness.

"Well, I'm sorry to disappoint ya, Mr. Pinder, but I do believe ya source is mistaken," I carefully stated, choosing each word as cautiously as a mother bird tending to her nearly hatched babies. "My brotha had nothin' to do with Ezra's disappearance."

I lowered my eyes, the verbal presence of Ezra's name bringing me to tears. Quickly though, I forcefully regrouped my emotion and boldly lifted my face back to Luke's.

"Now, if ya'd please excuse me, Mr. Pinder. I have my work to get back to."

Luke cleared his throat again and began to move toward the front of the store, when he spun quickly on his heels and returned to the counter. Before I could react, he dashed to the small entryway, the hinged, swinging half door the only solid barrier amid the few inches between us.

"I know you were in love with Mr. Washington," he whispered, his voice stern enough to seize my relentlessly chattering mind. "I know this because that's what I've been told and it's also what that look that is as clear as day on your face says. You loved—love this boy, and it is literally killing you that you can't find him."

Luke gripped my arm, the cold clamminess of his skin somehow warm and comforting.

"Help me, Judy," he pleaded, my eyes still fixed on the deli counter. "Help me find Ezra."

Tears began to flood my face and fall onto the counter below. Nodding, I turned toward Luke, the features of his face lost to the falling of water that blocked my vision and flooded my skin.

"Yes," I whispered, choking back a powerful sob of desperation. "Yes, I'll help you."

Luke patted my hand before retreating from the small swinging door.

"Good, Judy," he spoke, softly and carefully. "Meet me after your shift at the Clairmont Motel just outside of Waynesboro."

I wiped my eyes just in time to see him scan the area. Once certain we could not be heard, he continued.

"And don't tell a soul of where you're going."

I nodded, still mindful of my dripping face. I started to wipe my running nose with the corner of my apron, when Luke stepped toward me, his outreached hand holding the handkerchief from the front pocket of his jacket.

"I'll see you there, Judy."

With that, he darted from before the deli counter and out the front door of the store. For the rest of my shift, I focused silently on my work duties, careful to heed the spiraling warning of my brother's voice within my head, but in steadfast agreement with the prompting of my soul's own inner knowing, which subtly and gently assured me that I had made the right choice.

The front of the Clairmont Motel was not only quaint and charming, but also welcoming and inviting. I had never ventured inside before. The motel's location on the edge of town was very much off the beaten path of my usual routine.

I was just about to open the front door of the lobby, when a newly familiar voice called my name.

"Judy!"

I looked up to see Luke, now casual in a pair of khaki shorts and a button-down, short-sleeved shirt. He looked like he was on his way for a week-long vacation in Florida. I smiled and shuffled toward him.

"Glad you could make it," he smiled, pausing for a moment to allow our eyes to greet. "Follow me."

I turned my head nervously, afraid a suspicious or curious pair of eyes was watching us, but found no one. Quiet and obedient, I followed Luke down a narrow corridor, passing several bright red doors before finally reaching the sole open one. Once inside, Luke closed the door behind us, motioning for me to follow him toward the room's only dresser.

"I put together a little appetizer for us," he beamed, moving to the side so I could take in the sight of a small plate of cheese and crackers. Beside it: a bottle of red wine. Suddenly, I began to grow nervous regarding Luke's intentions. He must have sensed it because he quickly shuffled to fill the air with words of ease and comfort.

"Please don't be upset, Judy. I just thought it would be nice to provide some sort of snack. I know you've been working all day."

He brought his eyes to mine.

"As far as the red wine goes, well, it's not the romantic gesture you may be assuming. It's the only liquid I have in the room. Red wine is the only way I'm able to unwind at night. Sad as it is, it's the only way I can get to sleep."

Feeling a bit more secure, I reached for a cracker, carefully balancing the cheese as I moved the combination to my mouth. I could feel Luke smiling at me as I nervously scarfed it down.

"Sorry," I whispered shyly. "Ya right. I am hungry. I haven't eaten a thing all day."

He nodded.

"I assumed so. Sort of ironic, really. Handling food all day yet never consuming any. Must be torture."

I laughed.

"Well, Mr. Dolsan does allow me to swipe some of the nearly stale baked goods before he tosses 'em, but I just wasn't feelin' very hungry earlia'."

"Well, I'm happy that you are now."

He winked, passing me a paper cup filled with red wine. Hesitantly, I took it, allowing the warm liquid to graze my lips.

"Now," Luke said as he moved to the edge of the room's solo queen-sized bed, "you're correct that no crime has been committed regarding the disappearance of Ezra Washington."

I looked down at the bed, a neatly organized array of paperwork and documents decorating the plain blue bedspread. Now curious, I lifted my eyes back to Luke's.

"The truth of the matter is, Judy," Luke continued, lowering his eyes back to the mass of paper, adjusting some of the documents with the tips of his fingers. "The odds are incredibly high that something criminal has taken place involving Ezra. But let's not overlook the fact that outside of Ezra's disappearance, a crime has already been committed."

Confusion swirled over my expression.

"You were attacked, Judy. Raped."

The word jabbed into my side like a hunter's knife. I had still yet to understand that what had happened to me was truly criminal. A part of me simply refused to accept it, while most of me was far more concerned for Ezra to even care.

"We're going to get to the bottom of this, Judy. I promise you."

Luke spent the next half hour detailing to me the similar cases he had researched that had taken place all throughout the South. Not every case included an assault, but most centered around the mysterious disappearance of a young Negro male. My heart sank to the deepest depth of my core as Luke revealed the result of each and every case: murder. Not one of the young men he presented was ever found alive. Most were found hanging from a tree or buried in some tobacco field. Tears began to fall from my eyes and over the nearest documents as Luke methodically told his stories.

"Wait," he whispered, lifting my chin with his index finger. "Do you want to stop? Are you okay?"

I shook my head, the tears gushing faster down my cheeks. I struggled to breathe as Luke gently pulled me toward him. I focused on his subtle cologne, my face now pressed into his shirt.

Once I settled, Luke pulled me from his chest, allowing his eyes to ease over mine.

"We're going to get justice for this, Judy. No matter what happens. Whether we find Ezra or not, we are going to get justice."

The enormity of my emotion paralyzed my ability to react or speak, the reflection of my tear-stained face the only thing I could compute in the dimly lit mirror of Luke's bright blue eyes.

I finished off several more crackers and at least two more paper cups of wine before Luke requested what he needed of me.

"I'm going to need your cooperation, Judy," he spoke softly, carefully maneuvering his eyes over my face. "Most of the cases I just showed you went unprosecuted. Mostly due to the ignorance, bigotry, and racism of the juries, but also due to a lack of a willing and credible witness or witnesses."

He paused before continuing, assuring that his words were absorbed and understood.

"You are very important in all this, Judy," he spoke carefully, freezing his gaze over mine. "With your cooperation, we truly stand a chance at achieving some justice here."

I nodded, slowly comprehending what he was asking of me.

"Eventually, more evidence will appear and we can move forward with charges if need be."

He paused again, softly placing his hand over mine, which rested on the bed.

"Did your sheriff ever contact you? Did he take an official statement?"

Silent, I shook my head, the answer causing Luke to sigh disapprovingly.

"It's the same every time, I swear," he continued, more to himself than to me. "These backwoods sheriffs won't do a damn thing when it comes to anything to do with helping colored folk. Well, since the DA assigned me to the case, the sheriff and I are about to become real good friends."

I only listened, unsure how to respond. I agreed with everything Luke was saying, but as a lifelong resident of Waynesboro, Mississippi, I knew that the intensity of the racism of the Jim Crow South ran as strong and deep as the old-time religion. Most Southerners I knew believed the black man to be inferior just as much as they believed Jesus had risen from the dead. Some may agree that the unfair treatment wasn't right, even not very Christian, but they did little, if anything, to ever say a word to try to stop it. It was just accepted, every man and woman remaining firm and steady in their allotted and designated role in the agelong rules, both written and not, of the imperial South.

"Well," Luke continued, carefully stacking the now disheveled paper piles, "once we have enough evidence, or a body—"

He stopped, slowly lifting his eyes to mine.

I smiled, an instant, nervous response, and lowered my head back to my chest. I could cry no longer, and for whatever reason, the thought of Ezra no longer living was slowly becoming an emotionless and realistic possibility within my mind.

I followed Luke back to the front of the motel. By this point, the sun had begun its descent behind the towering Mississippi oak trees, the remaining embers of its glow sizzling atop the wooded skyline.

"You know I'm going to have to escort you home now," Luke stated as we turned to face each other in front of the sole door of the motel's lobby.

"No, it's all right," I responded, turning my head toward the darkened gravel pathway that would lead me back to town.

"Judy, no. I need—"

"It's okay, Luke, I swear."

I felt his hand cup over mine.

"I need to be able to fend for myself. I can't be all scared to walk alone in my own hometown."

"But, Judy," Luke whispered, following my eyes into the endless darkness beyond the faint glow of the motel's neon vacancy sign. "It is highly possible that the person who attacked you is still out there."

"I know," I replied without hesitating. "That's why I must travel alone."

I squeezed his hand and pulled away, ignoring his pleas as I ventured into the darkness.

With only the echo of Luke's voice behind me, and the security of his eyes fixed upon me, I journeyed into the night, unafraid and unfaltering in my bravery.

"Where ya been?" Francis demanded the moment I closed the cottage door behind me. "Ed is gonna be home any second, and ya know he'd be worried outta his mind if he knew ya was out there all alone after dark."

I didn't respond. I moved to the icebox, fetching the milk carafe and sipping from its side.

"Answer me, Judith. I ain't gonna stand for all this secrecy and whatnot. Were ya with that Yankee boy our brotha told ya to stay away from?"

"What's it to ya, Francis? Honestly?"

Francis's eyes widened at my defiance, her over-powdered face and lipstick-heavy mouth twisting into a snarl.

"Don't ya sass me that way, little miss!" she shouted, inching closer to me. "I'm ya sista. Ya flesh and blood. I deserve the common courtesy and respect ya give some stranga' on the street. The kinda courtesy and respect ya seem to give everyone these days."

"What's that s'posed to mean?" I scoffed. "What're ya tryin' to say?"

"I'm saying . . ." she faded into her mind, a tornado of thoughts and words clearly visible behind the windows of her eyes ". . . I'm saying that ya don't appear to be much of a lady by keepin' all this company lately. From the colored boy to this strange Yankee. People are gonna start to talk."

"People like you, right?" I seethed. "I swear, Francis, if ya cared about ya own business as much as ya do mine, ya'd be surprised at how busy ya'd be."

"How dare ya!" Francis screamed. "I'm just tryin' to look out for ya! I'm just tryin' to be sure ya safe. How's that so wrong?"

"I don't need ya lookin' after me, Francis. I'm a grown-ass woman. I'm ya older sista, need I remind ya. I certainly don't need my kid sista worryin' about my business."

I heard Francis laugh under her breath.

"Oh, ya don't, do ya?" she replied, her voice a low growl. "Well, how come ya is too damn stupid to realize what a wonderful thing ya got goin' for ya with Billy Jennings, but are too damn ignorant to accept and embrace it? Instead, ya gonna drive poor Billy away with all this nigga lovin' and Yankee doodlin' ya keep insistin' on doin'. Ya such a fool."

Tired of the argument, I turned my head from her direction, shifting my body to exit the kitchen.

It was then I heard my sister grab our largest and sharpest kitchen knife.

"Ya listen here and ya listen good," she hissed, halting my movement with the placement of the knife against my chest, the point of the blade just one slight movement from piercing my flesh. "Ya let go of worryin' about that damn nigga boy. I'll not warn ya of this again. If I see or hear that ya are still out there diggin' and pokin' around about him, I swear ta God, dear Sista, I'll cut ya down myself."

I stared at Francis, my eyes unblinking as I challenged her glare.

"I ain't afraid to do what needs to be done," she promised coldly.

I didn't speak, nor could I muster a word had I wanted to. I wasn't scared, nor was I angry. I was in shock. Pure and plain shock.

"Do ya understand me, Sista?"

She inched her face closer to mine, the knife now pricking into my skin, droplets of blood greeting the puncture of the blade tip.

I pinched my face into an angry scowl, my chin wobbling in defiance and emotion.

"I mean it," she whispered.

She dropped the knife, moved to the sink, and began washing the slight trickle of crimson blood from the dull silver of the blade. I stood firmly in place, the stinging of the small wound enhanced by the uneven heaving of my chest.

I turned to face Francis, when Ed opened the front door.

"What's the matta'?" he questioned, the sound of his voice heavy and concerned.

"Nothin', Ed," Francis replied from the sink, keeping her head in the direction of the water. "We was just havin' us a little sistaly discussion. Nothin' that concerns the brotha of the family."

I felt Ed's eyes graze across the back side of my head. I remained frozen in place, too afraid to turn toward him, exposing the trickle of blood that was running from between my breasts.

"Judy, ya okay?"

I closed my eyes, focused and intent to reply with a steady and firm voice.

"Yes, Ed," I said in a semi-whisper. "I'm fine."

Ed closed the front door behind him and began to walk toward the kitchen. Quickly, I moved forward and pressed a nearby dish towel against my wound.

Ed spun me around just as I did so.

"Ya had a day of it. I can tell."

His eyes fell over my face the way our father's used to. In a strange way, it was almost as if Daddy himself were peering at me lovingly through the open orbs of my brother's eyes.

"How about we get ya fed and into bed?"

I nodded, dropping my gaze from Ed's face in defeat and exhaustion.

I ate a bowl of soup alone while Ed and Francis, now on the front porch, embarked upon a heated yet muffled discussion.

I heard my name drop between them on more than several occasions, but I was now too tired and too unconcerned to bother trying to hear or make sense of the few words I could manage to make out.

Alone at the kitchen table, I finished off my canned soup and prepared myself for bed. I heard my siblings re-enter the house a few minutes later, the feeling of the Mississippi night air filling the space around me as I fell into a deep yet restless sleep.

No one would speak to me when I arrived for work the next morning. In fact, I swore I saw several passersby on the street purposely turn their faces from my direction as I walked. Something was the matter, its presence alive and nearly tangible in the damp humidity of the Mississippi morning.

Mr. Dolsan would only speak to me when it was a necessary matter of work-related importance. Otherwise, he too kept a silent distance.

Finally, around noon, I walked over to Branson, the store clerk, and asked him what was going on.

"Why is everyone actin' so strange, Branson?"

He peeked at me nervously over his shoulder, careful not to turn his head completely. Slowly, he returned to the shelf he was tending to, acting as if he had not heard me speaking to him.

"Branson!" I said louder, the unexpected bark of my voice causing the young boy to jump in place, his shoulder nearly touching his ears in fright.

"Uh . . ." he mumbled, the cracking of his puberty-stricken voice slowly finding its way from his spot-covered face and throat.

He rose to his feet, the height between us equal, yet our ages nearly a decade apart. I watched as he lowered his eyes toward the corner of the store's front door, his gaze stopping once it hit the wire bin that held the daily newspaper.

I followed his gaze, moving toward the door slowly and steadily.

The rack was on the outside of the glass, yet I could clearly read the giant bold and black letters of the headline. I fell to my knees as each word seared into my brain.

"Headless Negro Corpse Found in Wayne County Creek."

I screamed, a scream so powerful and unrecognizable that even my own ears flinched at the sound. I dropped my face against the glass, the streaking of fingerprints and tears sliding beneath my skin as I slid my body back and forth.

I could see several pairs of feet stop on the sidewalk, the feeling of several pairs of eyes draping over me at once.

More than one person lifted me from the ground, but only one person was recognizable beyond the flood of water and matted hair that clouded my eyes: Luke.

I fell into his arms, my chest shuddering in an uncontrollable heaving.

Luke wrapped his arms around me, squeezing me as tightly as he could in an attempt to provide me some form of comfort.

"They killed him, Luke!" I screamed, my voice so shrill and high that even I didn't recognize it. "They killed him!"

I could hear Luke hushing me softly, the run of his hand over the back of my head both irritating and disturbing.

"No!" I bellowed, my throat burning and raw from anger. "Don't try and shush me!"

Luke attempted to speak, but I stopped him.

"Ya knew about this! Ya've known! How long did ya know, Luke? When were ya gonna tell me?"

Luke shook his head but was again cut short of his words before they were even spoken.

"Why, Luke? Why?"

I fell into his arms again; this time, the countless pairs of shoes beyond the glass were now clearly visible through the small space between Luke's arm and chest. I was a spectacle, a sideshow, my obvious and overwhelming pain some street-side entertainment the people of Waynesboro were curiously and willingly lapping up.

"What?" I screamed, ripping myself from Luke's grasp. "What're y'all looking at?"

The clouded faces of the nearby onlookers began to move and shuffle, most turning and walking away, but some standing firm in their place of open gawking.

"Y'all love this, don't ya? The dumb white girl who dared to love a black boy. Ya love this!"

Luke gripped my shoulders. I heard Mr. Dolsan whispering something behind me. Before I could say more, the pull-down shade of the store's front door and window were being lowered, a terrified-looking Branson quickly pulling them into place.

I continued to sob as Luke led me toward the back of the store. He closed the door to the storage room and sat beside me.

"Hey," he whispered, his face only inches from mine, the now familiar, faint scent of his cologne filling the air. "We don't know anything for certain yet, Judy. The body has yet to be identified."

I wasted no time in replying, lifting my face to Luke's the way a cobra sizes up its prey.

"Do ya think I'm stupid, Luke?" I spoke softly, the burden of my words heavy and cumbersome through my throat. "Of course it's him."

Luke seemed uncertain as to how to reply. He shook his head and attempted to wrap his arms around me.

"No!" I shouted, my voice stern and hollow. "No!"

I felt my eyes spin in a crazed dizziness, the reflection of my face blurred and unidentifiable in the blue curvature of his eyes.

Luke didn't speak another word for the next twenty minutes or so. He gently held my hand as I sobbed uncontrollably, the vision of Ezra's smiling face appearing in the darkness behind my eyes, its solo presence both aching and comforting.

I was too incoherent by the time Francis appeared in the doorway of the storage room. I didn't reply nor resist as she carefully led me out the back door of Dolsan's Grocery. I saw Luke watching from the alleyway as Francis continued to lead me in the direction of home, her hand gripped firmly against my shoulder.

Francis never uttered a word as we journeyed in silence. Only the sound of my relentless and methodical sobbing filled the space between us. I collapsed once we passed the threshold of the front door, the feeling of the splinter-heavy floorboards slamming into my face the last conscious memory I had before fading into darkness.

4

Ya Gonna Need Me, Judy

Sheriff John Roberts Jr. stood over six feet tall, a potbelly the size of a beer keg, and a receding hairline that ducked beneath his large-brimmed cowboy hat. The people of Waynesboro never referred to him by either of his proper names. We simply called him Sheriff. He headed the town's only law enforcement. In fact, Wayne County only had a three-man sheriff's department. Waynesboro was still too small to afford its own police department, so Sheriff ruled the roost and oversaw each and every facet of the various minor and often petty legal issues of the town. This was a murder though, a brutal, cold-blooded killing that not only shook the very core of Waynesboro, but also forced Sheriff and his two deputies into the forefront of the national media.

"When was the last time ya physically saw Ezra Washington?" Sheriff asked, his bright green eyes magnified by copper-framed bifocals. I could see the subtle sweat beading over his brow as he nervously shuffled through the pile of papers he clutched in his white-knuckled fists.

The Wayne County Sheriff's Office was a turn-of-the-century downtown building that had withstood various local fires, the side winds of a passing violent tornado, even an infamous flood that had washed out the very foundation of nearly every original structure in downtown Waynesboro.

"I believe it was the day prior to the . . ." my words trailed along with my eyes as they toured the contents of Sheriff's large and overdecorated office. Plaques and trophies lined the walls and window sills; large-framed photographs of Sheriff attending various town and state events peppered over the fading white wallpaper. The room appeared as a shrine to one man's ego rather than a proper sheriff's workspace. Still, despite the pomp and circumstance of his character, Sheriff was a devoted and passionate public servant of Waynesboro, and the townspeople revered and adored him for it.

"The day afta'—go on, sweet girl. I need for ya to detail everything as best as possible."

I had never witnessed Sheriff so jumpy and disorganized before. It was incredibly clear that the enormity of the crime committed was far beyond anything Sheriff had ever encountered, much less spearheaded an investigation of, in his entire twenty-plus-year career.

"Honestly, Sheriff, I really can't recall. Everything has become so very hazy to me now . . . I just remember . . ."

"Dammit, Judith, I understand this is all very upsettin'. But I got a dead colored boy on my hands and half the country's newspapers on my ass for more information. I gotta make sure we have all our ducks in a row."

I stared at Sheriff. The disbelief that he cared more about looking good in the situation instead of the tragic and brutal details of the loss of a local life was flabbergasting to me.

"I'm sorry, Sheriff," I continued slowly, more out of concern than fear. "I'll try and remember more detail. I'm just . . . I'm still just . . ."

"We'll talk more lata', Judith," Sheriff said, shaking his head in clear and visible disappointment. "Right now, I've got that damn

Yankee assistant DA comin' by for yet anotha' meetin'. Ya should get outta here before he arrives. I'm sure he'd have himself a big-city-boy hissy fit if he knew I had ya down here without him bein' present. Not to mention ya brotha was here yesterday . . . also without the Yankee. The last thing I need is for him to start makin' trouble for me too. The goddamn newspapa' folk are doin' a mighty fine job of that as it is."

I watched as he turned from his desk chair and moved to a large filing cabinet.

"I swear to God, ya'd think these people ain't neva' seen a damn dead nigga before."

Emotionlessly, I excused myself from Sheriff's office and nervously shuffled back to the front of the building. Ed was waiting for me in his work truck. He had followed us here after Sheriff had arrived at the house to retrieve me for questioning. Sheriff had taken Ed in for questioning the day prior. Despite the latest circumstances, I had obeyed Ed's earlier command to never bring up or mention the topic again. I had yet to say a word to him about the body, or Ezra, or any inkling of suspicion or thought I may have had regarding my brother's involvement or participation in what more than likely happened to my Ezra. It had only been two days since the discovery of the body, and the town was aflame with rumor and speculation. I, on the other hand, was barely able to breathe, much less eat or function properly. Even my usual routine in the bathroom had changed, my body expelling the lower fluids of my intestines with each pang and twitch of overwhelming despair and nervousness. Though nothing had yet been confirmed, I just knew in the inner depths of the very heart of my soul that it was indeed Ezra's headless corpse they had dragged from the solid muck of a nearby Mississippi creek.

Besides the long visits to the toilet, I hadn't left my bed since Francis brought me home from Dolsan's. When I wasn't expelling my bowels or vomiting stomach bile, I was endlessly crying, only a few futile bouts of unconsciousness slightly easing the constant pain in my core or the rambling chatter of my brain.

"How'd it go?" Ed asked nervously as I slowly slid my body over the tattered leather bench seat of the truck cab.

"Not well," I replied, using every bit of strength I had left to pull the heavy truck door shut. "I don't rememba' all the detail he wants from me. All I rememba' is that I was . . . that thing happened in the woods and . . . I just—"

"It's okay, Judy," Ed interrupted, the touch of his hand on mine soft and comforting. "He's the law. He'll figya it out with or without ya."

I couldn't help but notice how rapidly Ed was adjusting his usual gob of chewing tobacco. Where it usually remained flat and firm against his lower gums, the black wad now flipped and slid between his lips and lower teeth in a rhythmic and grotesque cycle. I could hardly look at him while he spoke, the saliva-drenched mush too distracting and stomach turning for me to bear.

I headed straight for bed once we returned home, not even glancing over at Francis, who had immediately run to the front door the very second we started up the gravel pathway to the house.

I could hear her and Ed whispering out on the front porch, my name again a heavy topic of their conversation. Yet, once again, I was too physically and emotionally exhausted to even try to fuse together or make sense of the bits and pieces I could clearly hear and understand. Reluctantly, I gave way to much-needed sleep.

The sun was down when I finally awoke, the sound of various voices echoing from beyond the front door. Carefully, I inched my way to the living room window, cautiously peeking through the blue lace curtain and out to the front porch. There, I saw the Benson brothers, their oil-stained and tattered work shirts matching, the only difference between them the lengths of their burning cigarettes.

"That lawya' that's down here from up North had Sheriff bring us in so he could ask us a bunch'a questions," I heard Ron Benson, the younger of the two brothers, and by all accounts, the smartest, say. "Separately, too."

"I'll bet it was them niggas we roughed up that gave 'em our names . . . unless it was Judy," Fred Benson interjected, the lack of education beyond the fourth grade painful and obvious the more he spoke. "Frannie, ya said ya had told her in the hospital that Ed and us was out lookin' for the boy? Ya think she told Sheriff and that lawya' our names?"

"None of that matta's anyways. They ain't even gonna be able to identify that body," Ron continued, the high school graduate between the two, but no more sophisticated than his simple-minded older brother. The Benson boys were who you went to when you needed some brute force to lift a heavy piece of furniture or install a new car radiator. They certainly weren't sought after in regard to their intelligence, be it country smarts or otherwise.

"Look, the body was found in Wayne County, so that means any potential trial will take place here," I heard Francis say, her words the most firm and certain of the bunch. "Even with that Yankee boy involved, between Billy's daddy as attorney general, Sheriff's involvement, and the townsfolk of Waynesboro as the jury, there ain't no one in their right mind gonna send some white boys to jail for protectin' a white woman."

"But you said Judy is goin' aroun' sayin' it wasn't that boy who raped her . . . That might make it more of an interest to the papers and whatnot. They ain't gonna leave this be till there's an arrest."

I watched in a heart-pounding, breathless silence as Ron Benson concluded his words by taking one final drag of his cigarette and flicking it over the wooden railing of the front porch. It was when his eyes met mine that my entire being seemed to paralyze and cease operation completely.

"Hey, shh," he hissed at the rest of the group, who, besides Ed, continued to talk over one another.

I dropped the curtain and started to tiptoe back to the bed. I heard the bodies on the front porch begin to move and scatter. The sound of the front door opening caused me to leap the last foot or so. I was just pulling the covers over my body, when Francis snatched the curtain that separated our bedroom area from Ed's and the rest of the house.

"What did ya hear?" she asked coldly, the inflection of her voice confirming that she was in no mood to entertain the possibility that I may truly be sleeping.

I opened my eyes and peered at her, too shocked by the front porch conversation to resist confronting her.

"I heard enough to know that y'all had somethin' to do with this," I spoke softly, my voice littered and broken by a quiet stream of fresh tears.

"Ain't nobody out there admittin' to nothin', Sista," she continued, validating her words with a gleaming fire of certainty in her eyes. "We just simply sayin' that whoeva' done took care of this boy ain't gonna haveta face some long punishment. Justice was served."

She inched closer to me, the pungent aroma of what I assumed was the Benson boys' moonshine heavy on her breath.

"And there ain't gonna be no problem unless you keep goin' aroun' sayin' ya don't think it was that colored boy who attacked ya."

She sat on the bed, gripping her left hand onto my right wrist.

"Whad'ya tell Sheriff?" she whispered, the smell of the moonshine so intense that I could almost taste it.

"I didn't tell him that," I responded, still in shock and now starting to panic. "What difference does it make what I say? The fact of the matta' is, there is a dead boy out there, and someone is gonna haveta pay the price for that."

Francis's eyes spun and glimmered in the dim light of the room, the powerful liquor now seeming to ooze from around her lids.

"Ya so stupid, Judy," she laughed, easing her grip on my wrist. "Someone done paid for it already. That nigga boyfriend of yours. He paid the price for rapin' ya."

She hesitated for a moment, the darkness of her thoughts now clouding her eyes and burdening the tone of her voice.

"I bet ya wanted it, didn't ya?" she whispered, bringing her face just an inch or so from mine. "I bet ya loved that nigga cock slidin' all up inside ya."

I didn't say a word as my right fist lifted from beneath the blankets and pummeled into Francis's left cheek. Without a bit of resistance, she fell to the floor, much of her weight landing on her right shoulder.

"Ya dumb nigga lova'," she laughed. "Our daddy is rollin' in his grave right now. If he were still alive, ya'd be the death of him for sure."

"Stop it, Francis!" I screamed, lowering my legs to the floor and inching toward her. I raised my right foot and held it over her head. "Say one more word . . . anything, and I swear on Daddy's grave that I'll crush ya skull in."

She continued to laugh, the darkness in her eyes now so dense and heavy it eliminated any of the white. In the shadows between us, she appeared like a demon, dark, soulless pits now in place where her sky-blue eyes once were.

I felt myself giving in to the urge to kick her, when Ed appeared from behind the curtain.

"Hey!" he commanded our attention. "Enough!"

Obeying, I lowered my leg and sat on the edge of the bed.

"Get off the floor, Francis. Go wash up. Ya need to get ya drunk ass in bed."

Slowly, Francis pushed herself from the floor, slurring her continuous laughter at me as she stammered to her full height.

"Nigga lova'," she mouthed, keeping her fiery eyes locked on mine.

I closed my eyes and allowed her to pass, hearing Ed assist her to the small bathroom sink. Moments later, he reappeared.

"Hey," he said softly, slowly making his way to the bedside. "There a lot of people concerned for ya and what happened to this boy. Ya just need to get ya rest and allow everything to take its course. Stop worryin' about it all."

Tears began to drift down my face again. Just when I thought I could cry no longer, somehow, my body found a hidden reservoir of water buried deep within me, piercing its walls and allowing yet more salt-laced liquid to cover my skin.

"Enough, Judy," Ed whispered, gently pushing me down in the bed. "Just rest. Don't worry about what Francis says. Just ignore her."

I didn't respond or argue. I allowed my brother to tuck me in, accepted his soft, gentle kiss to my temple, and awaited the inevitable arrival of my inebriated sister.

"Nigga lova', nigga lova', nigga lova'," she repeated in a singsong whisper as she crawled to her space on the bed, keeping her voice just loud enough for me to hear.

Taking Ed's advice, I ignored her. I pictured Ezra's face as I prayed to God above to somehow give me the truth, all the while assuring my sanity as I awaited it.

I had become a prisoner to the cottage over the next few days. My first and only attempt to return to work failed miserably, when a set of three reporters from various places in the nation bombarded me while I attempted to hide behind the deli counter. I broke down as they hurled their invasive questions at me. My emotionally weighted reaction caused Mr. Dolsan to arrange a ride home for me. He stated that I remain there at least until the growing interest in the case had settled. It was only growing worse though. The gathering of curious out-of-town onlookers and growing numbers of newspaper journalist and reporters now clogged the gravel pathway to our house. Ed had tried several times to shoo them away with the presence of Daddy's shotgun, but nothing seemed to deter the interest as the days slowly morphed into weeks. On exactly the one-month anniversary of the discovery of the body, Sheriff, along with both deputies, arrived to arrest Ed.

I watched from the kitchen window as my only brother was handcuffed and escorted to Sheriff's Ford police car. I stood without emotion, whereas Francis threw herself on the ground before the car. The spectacle caused the gathered onlookers and reporters to shout and interject, their flashbulbs popping and cameras clicking as the two deputies lifted Francis from the ground and returned her to the front porch. Only Luke Pinder remained as the crowd of curious townsfolk, various onlookers, and flustered local and national reporters were ushered back behind the police-constructed barrier at the foot of the gravel driveway.

Luke and I met eyes, staring at one another for what felt like hours before he finally motioned for me to come to the door. Francis stormed past me without a word as Luke appeared in the doorway.

"Based on our witness testimony, I was able to get a grand jury to indict your brother and both Benson brothers for the murder of Ezra Washington."

I turned from the doorway and walked silently to the kitchen table. I could cry no longer. I could no longer react. I simply remained soundless, the absorption of the latest developments swirling around in my head in a migraine-inducing whirlwind.

"This is great news, Judy," Luke continued, closing the front door and following me to the kitchen table. "After Ms. Washington was finally given permission to identify what was left of the body, I was able to move forward with a grand jury proceeding."

I peered up at Luke's excited and beaming face, my pathetic reflection shimmering in the glint of his enthusiastic eyes. Without a sound, I dropped my weight onto my usual chair at the table, my arms hanging lifelessly at my side, my oily and matted hair dropping and sticking to my greasy face. I hadn't bathed in at least a week; the unpleasant odor of my flesh, both hidden and exposed, was starting to gag even me.

"Judy . . ." Luke said softly, sliding a chair close to mine. "We may actually get some justice here. The fact that I was able to get a Wayne County grand jury to indict three of their own white men for the murder of a black man certainly says a lot. I mean, sure, there was an indictment by a grand jury in the Till murder, too, but I think a lot of Mississippians now feel guilty and embarrassed over the way that murder trial was handled. Especially when just less than a year after they were acquitted, the two men charged with the murder admitted their guilt to a magazine for money. Because of that, perhaps this time a jury will be more willing to look past any prejudices and deliver a verdict based on the law. Murder is murder. A heinous crime. Not to mention an immoral one. It doesn't matter the circumstances surrounding it, such as the guilt of the victim or the personal righteousness of the perpetrators, and most certainly not race. Taking the law into one's hands is not the way our society or justice system works. I would think that most good people would agree that any man taking another man's life is wrong, regardless of the reason, and that a legal punishment is validated."

He lifted his arm and slowly placed a hand over mine. His touch caused me to raise my head and force my voice from its locked encasement.

"But, my brotha," I rasped, my voice rough and hollow from days of not speaking. "What'll happen to him?"

Seemingly stunned by my reaction, Luke cleared his throat and repositioned himself on the chair.

"Well, that's for a jury to decide," he confirmed nervously. "We have several witnesses who all claim to have seen Ed and the Benson brothers together on that night, aggressively searching for Ezra in the colored section of town. They report being manhandled and questioned by the trio as the boys actively combed the entire area. Unfortunately, or perhaps at this point, fortunately, Billy Jennings is refusing to testify. I could subpoena him, but Billy's witness statement does not corroborate Ed's statement that Billy was the one to tell Ed that it was Ezra he had pulled off you in the attack. This would certainly work against us in trying to establish a clear motive for the murder, so I would rather just leave him out. Thankfully, from the last I've heard, the defense isn't going to subpoena him either. I feel confident that my set of witnesses will be enough to convince the jury that it was indeed Ed and the Bensons who committed this murder. It was effective on the grand jury, and that proceeding was missing a vital witness: the victim of the attack that initiated the murder—you, Judy."

I moved my eyes over Luke's, my brokenness and heartache too powerful and weighted for me to muster another response. I dropped my head to my chest, the effort required to continue facing Luke far too demanding on the fledgling reserves of my depleted energy.

"Whaddya want here?" I heard Francis's voice break the silence. "Are ya here 'cause ya plannin' on representin' our brotha?"

From the top corner of my eyes, I could see Luke spin on his chair to face my sister, her face swollen and red with emotion.

"Uh, hello, Francis," Luke fumbled. "Uh, no, ma'am. I was appointed by the Tenth Circuit Court district attorney to oversee the disappearance and now murder case of Ezra Washington. I'm assistant DA Luke Pinder."

Slowly, I lifted my head just as Francis stormed into Luke's face.

"Ya get outta here!" she screamed, her voice sounding as though it had broken the very limits of its physical existence and strength.

I watched in a faded haze as Francis forcefully pulled at Luke's brown suit jacket, ignoring his cutoff pleas for her understanding.

Having none of it, I dropped my head back to my chest just as Francis shoved Luke out the front door, slamming it so hard, several picture frames crashed from various walls of the cottage, cracking and shattering on the floor in unison.

I could hear her sobbing in the slight distance between us, the silhouette of her hunched and defeated shoulders visible in the upper vision of my eyes. I didn't say a word as I sat steadfast in my chair, the migraine worsening with each pulsating beat of my heart.

Moments later, I felt Francis inching toward me, the shuffle of her feet over the worn floorboards of the cottage haunting and ominous as she neared me.

"What we gonna do, Judy?" she sobbed, her weak and feeble reaction in stark contrast to what I had been expecting from her. "Ed's in jail."

Somehow trusting her current demeanor, I lifted my face to meet hers, an early childhood memory from around the time we had first lost Daddy dancing into my mind as I took in the terrified and emotionally defeated face of my sister. The stained and imprinted memory of my sister's face the day we had gathered in the local cemetery to lower our father's coffin into the ground reappeared before my eyes as if it were happening all over again. For the first time in my life since that day, I felt instantly and deeply connected to my sister, an emotional and psychological bond of compassion and understanding fusing between us in an unspoken, unseen, and powerful way.

Without a word or hesitation, I lifted my arm and embraced Francis's right wrist. Instantly, she fell into my chest, her entire body collapsing on top of me with sudden force and weight. I blacked out slightly as we both toppled from the chair and onto the floor beside the table. My sister's hair fell into my eyes and mouth as I struggled to catch my breath. Instead of attempting to resist her in any way, I simply closed my arms around her, collecting her heaving sobs into my core as the minutes passed into more than an hour. It was only when I felt Francis's chest begin to rise and fall with the automatic rhythm of unconsciousness, that I slowly rolled her from on top of me and to the open space of floor beside us. I didn't try to move or rise from the floor. I simply lay still next to my softly sleeping sister, watching the last rays of sunlight fade and flicker into the shadows of the ceiling.

Sheriff returned early the next morning. Both Francis and I were sitting at the table, attempting to eat our individual plates of eggs and toast. In a rare instance, Sheriff removed his hat as he took a seat at the kitchen table, his graying, receding brown hair collecting golden bits of morning sunlight as the massive, fiery orb began its ascent over the trees that edged the line of our property. Francis and I listened to him silently as he detailed the latest developments.

"Well, girls," Sheriff sighed, hungrily eyeing the barely touched food on our plates. "It looks as though this whole mess is goin' to trial. It seems it was that missin' colored boy's momma that called the DA's office. That's why that Yankee boy was sent down here before I even had a chance to run the law in my own county. She and her younga' son, along with two other colored boys around the same age, are the state's witnesses. Their witness testimony was enough evidence for the grand jury to indict."

Francis offered Sheriff her toast as I looked on in silence.

"For the life of me, I can't understand how a group of our own good people would ever allow for some loudmouthed niggas to accuse a stand-up white man such as your brotha. I mean, that boy was an animal, like all those nigga men are. I can't believe some of our own townsfolk is overlookin' the fact that a young white girl lost her innocence in all this. Who cares what happened to the boy after that? Goddamn, I wish I knew who was on that grand jury."

I felt Sheriff's eyes ease over my face. I focused on my plate, the mixture of yellow scrambled eggs and slightly burnt white toast fading into a blur of colorless nothing in front of me.

"Are you okay, shugga?" I heard Sheriff ask. "I know ya been goin' through hell. I'm so sorry ya brotha has to be accused in all this. No matter what happened, Ed was only tryin' to protect his sista. That's a God-given right as far as I'm concerned. Nigga or no nigga."

I didn't speak nor react as Sheriff continued to fill the heavy silence of the room with pointless and useless rhetoric of Southern pride and tradition. Even Francis appeared to tune him out as she methodically poked her fork at the rubbery eggs on her plate. It wasn't until Sheriff finally excused himself that my sister and I dared to speak to each other.

"Ed is guilty, isn't he?" I asked, keeping my eyes locked on my plate.

Francis didn't reply. She rose from her chair and shuffled slowly to the kitchen sink.

"Francis," I continued, raising my voice to assert my persistence, "tell me what ya know. Did Ed have anything to do with all this?"

She ignored me, purposely and loudly clanking each plate and utensil together in an obvious attempt to silence my voice.

"Francis!"

There was a knock at the front door. I watched as Francis silently shuffled to answer it, refusing to look my way, much less acknowledge my words with any form of response.

"Hey, Francis," I heard Billy Jennings's voice say. "How ya holdin' up?"

I collected my plate and delivered it to the kitchen sink, when I heard Billy say my name.

"Hey, Judy," he spoke in a semi-whisper, standing in the kitchen beside Francis in a duo of staring faces. "Are you okay?"

"Someone I cared for is dead, and my brotha is to blame for it," I stated coldly, watching my words drift over both my sister and Billy. Curiously, Billy's face twisted slightly at the mention of Ezra. A fiery gleam I had never witnessed on him before danced in his eyes, raging and vibrant. Startled, I cocked my head curiously.

"What is it ya want, Billy? I already done told ya that I don't need anything from ya."

"Yes, ya do," he answered instantly, the same fiery gleam still overpowering his gaze.

"Wha—"

"Ya best rememba' who it is I am," Billy interrupted.

I looked at Francis. Instead of her usual, intense glare, the solemn, cold, and silent look from the night before remained draped over her face.

"My daddy is the state attorney general. Top law a'the land," Billy continued, his eyes locked on my face. "That means ya gonna need my help."

I looked at Billy, his face glowing in the now fully risen sunlight. Francis continued to gaze in my direction, but her blank expression detailed a lack of coherence or attention. I returned my eyes to Billy.

"What're ya talkin' about, Billy?" I asked, allowing my natural annoyance with him to accent and decorate my voice.

"What I mean, Judy," he started, turning his head toward Francis and then back to me, "is that my daddy can influence how this whole thing turns out."

I didn't speak as Billy's words absorbed into my brain; fresh and potent.

"If ya brotha indeed had a hand in this colored kid's murda' . . ."

I watched as his face sank into a shadowy space just outside of the kitchen window's sun-emblazoned spotlight.

"Well, with all these damn Yankee reporta's here and such, it could spell a world a'trouble for ya brotha."

Billy inched toward me, his face still darkened by both the shadows and his suddenly sinister expression.

"It ain't gonna be so easy gettin' a white man off for rightfully puttin' a colored boy in his place with all these Yankee eyes on us."

Billy stood before me now, his tongue pinched between his front teeth. The faint scent of his aftershave wafted over my face, the fired glint of his eyes now so close I could make out the detail of the flaming embers.

"Ya gonna need me, Judy," he whispered, his breath sweet with the smell of mouthwash. "I know ya gonna wanna save ya brotha. I might be the only way."

I started to respond, when there was another knock at the front door. The presence of Sheriff entering the cottage absorbed the darkened and heavy atmosphere that had suddenly engulfed the entire space around us.

"Well, hey, Bill," Sheriff said as he closed the door behind him, limping slightly as he made his way to the kitchen. "Is everything okay?"

Instantaneously, Billy's face morphed from dark and sinister to bright and welcoming. His much sought-after charm lit the room around him, easily overpowering the golden rays of the sun.

"Hey, Sheriff," Billy chimed, his voice booming and vibrant. "I just came by to check on the girls."

"Good man," Sheriff smiled, patting Billy on the shoulder.

"Well, I no sooner got back to the office, when that damn Yankee boy asked for ya."

Sheriff's eyes ventured over mine.

"I'm sorry, Judy," Sheriff continued, his expression dropping. "I have no choice but to take ya back down to see him. Apparently, he needs some more information from ya."

My eyes jumped over the various faces of the room. Francis continued to stare blankly, whereas Billy's eyes again sparked and twinkled under the weight of his newly presented fire-like gaze. I forced my eyes back to Sheriff's.

"Fine," I agreed. "Just let me wash up and change."

Billy's smile pulled to the right side of his face as he watched me exit the room. In the distance, I could hear both Sheriff and Billy quietly discussing the case. Ed's name, as well as my own, echoed and repeated over the course of their conversation as I hurriedly spot-washed my body and face, pulling my hair into a single ponytail.

Billy stood beside Francis on the front porch as I joined Sheriff on the front bench seat of his Ford. I couldn't help but take in Billy's still twisted and sinister-looking face, a look and energy I had ever yet to witness, on him or any other human being.

The frozen image of Billy's face caused my stomach to lurch and shudder as Sheriff turned the car toward the main road and floored the accelerator. My brain began to echo what I was dreading the most: what if Ed were guilty? Would I ever be able to find in my heart the ability to forgive him, much less the courage to actually ask Billy Jennings to somehow intervene to save his life?

I couldn't get over the number of people waiting for us to arrive at the sheriff's office. Newspaper reporters shouted questions at me as Sheriff opened the passenger-side door of the police car and escorted me inside.

"It's gettin' worse every day, I swear. Every hour, at least three to five more reporta's show up. The only good thing in all this is how great this is for the motels and restaurants here in Waynesboro."

Sheriff concluded his statement by ushering me into his office and closing the door.

"No matta' what ya give these people, it's never enough. I swear, they want ya to provide a judge, jury, and verdict all on the very first day. I can't even sleep or shit without these damn reporta's snoopin' in my business."

I smiled nervously as Sheriff continued to both speak out loud and mumble to himself while cutting and lighting a cigar.

"Now, honey," he started, leaning over his desk in order to speak softly. "I fibbed a bit so I could get ya back here alone. That Yankee boy didn't ask for ya. I know he's headin' up this whole investigation and all, but this is a personal matta'. Judy, I've known ya since the day you was born. Hell, I'as playin' pool with ya daddy the day ya momma gave birth to Ed. Now with ya daddy gone and ya momma run off, I care for you kids the way I would if ya was my own. It hurts me to know I couldn't protect ya from somethin' so terrible. It's my job to protect ya, this town, this whole damn county. Baby girl, I'd give anything to go back and stop this from happenin' to ya. Please, for my own peace'a mind, tell me exactly what happened that night."

I looked away nervously, the very mention of the attack conjuring uncomfortable and unclear, hazy images. I took a deep breath in an attempt to calm my vastly growing nerves.

"I know this is difficult for ya, sweetheart, but please."

"I . . ." I stumbled, my voice cracking from the pressure of emotion and nerves. "I only remember . . . the rain. It was raining."

"Okay, good," Sheriff coaxed, the burning tip of his cigar filling the room with a warm and sweet fragrance.

"I was hit from behind. Knocked to the ground and pulled into the woods."

"All right, by who?"

"I don't know. I didn't see a face."

I could feel Sheriff's eyes darting over my downturned head. Forcefully, I held back welling tears.

"Did ya hear anything? Did someone speak to ya?"

"No," I continued, sucking in cigar-smoke-heavy air with nearly every word. "I did hear one voice though. I couldn't make out much of the words, but I recognized the voice."

"Who was it?" Sheriff asked, resting the still-burning cigar over a massive crystal ashtray.

"It was Ezra," I said plainly, no emotion in my voice.

"All right then," Sheriff nodded, leaning back in his chair. "That's what I needed to confirm."

"But . . ." I spoke breathlessly. "He . . . I know he . . . I don't believe he . . ."

"Listen, dear girl," Sheriff interrupted. "It's becomin' known how ya fancied this boy."

I looked up, expecting condemnation and judgment, but instead received only a look of sympathy and apparent understanding.

"I understand ya don't want to believe someone ya cared for would do somethin' like that to ya, but the fact of the matta' is, no colored male can be trusted around white females. It's just the facts, honey. I don't have no personal issue with the coloreds, but I been at this job long enough to know that a Negro male has primal instincts and urges that he simply cannot harness nor control. It was only a matta' a'time before this happened to ya."

Sheriff held my full attention with the relentless grip of his eyes. I absorbed his words without resistance or defiance.

"It's sorta like havin' a rattlesnake as a pet," he continued, lifting his cigar and replacing it to the corner of his mouth. "Ya may be able to feed and care for it for some time. Hell, ya may even believe the damn thing likes ya, or is ya friend. But the truth is pure science and factual. A rattler is eventually gonna bite ya, and it's hard to feel sorry for ya when it does. It's just in its blood to do so."

"It's not like that, Sheriff," I whispered, my words weighted and heavy. "Ezra was kind. He was my friend. We cared very much for each other."

Observing me as I spoke, Sheriff rhythmically puffed his cigar as the wheels in his head visibly turned behind his peering eyes.

"Listen here, Judy," he commanded, leaning back over the desk. "Whatever thing ya had goin' with this colored boy is your business. But be goddamn sure that once the press gets wind a'this, it ain't gonna be an easy ride for ya. Especially given the outcome."

I watched silently as he stood from his chair and limped to my side of the desk.

"This whole thing is only gonna prove why the Negroes haveta be contained to their own areas a'society. We can't just have these animals walkin' around among us. It's just the natural orda' a'things."

Sheriff placed his hands over my shoulders, his grip both sooth-ing and cold.

"Ya gonna haveta realize and accept that it was ya innocence and dignity that was sacrificed to prove this point. If ya brotha and the Benson boys took care of this nigga, it was only to protect ya. That is how it'll be seen by the press . . . even the damn Yankees."

I wanted to cry, but could only breathe.

"Now, our focus must remain on ya brotha. Jim Hemming is headin' up the defense team, pro bono. They in good hands with ol' Jim."

I stood from my chair and began to follow Sheriff toward the door.

"This is all about to get real ugly, Judy," Sheriff stated, still grip-ping my shoulders. "But ya haveta remember, with all this national interest and all, one wrong word or move and ya brotha could go down for this. It's hard to believe that is even possible given the circumstances, but the world is startin' to change. No more do people of this great country understand and accept that the coloreds are not the same as us. They haveta be treated and controlled differently. Some Yankee press is suggestin' that what was done to that boy was inhumane, unjustified, and criminal. But we know betta'. We know a nigga boy who attacks and assaults a white woman cannot be reintroduced into society or rehabilitated as some suggest. There is only one surefire way to alleviate the problem, and that remedy may have already been administa'd. I know we talk like the body we found is for sure this boy, but till we locate a head, there ain't nothin' for certain."

Sheriff lifted his hand to touch my cheek.

"But just in case, don't be goin' around talkin' about how ya was friends with this boy, or how ya think he cared for ya, sweet girl. Talk like that will only distract from the matta' at hand."

Sheriff patted my head and smiled.

"Ya a good girl, Judy. I imagine ya might be forgiven for some youth-ignorant nigga lovin'."

Suddenly, his face became stern and cold.

"But ya won't be forgiven for turnin' ya own brotha in as a murdera'. I don't care what anyone says, if ya brotha did indeed have a hand in takin' care'a that boy, if that's what even happened, his actions woulda been outta love and protection for his sista."

He cupped his hand under my jaw, lifting my face until our noses were only an inch or less apart.

"Ya honor ya race, dear girl. Ya stick by ya blood."

He dropped my face but waited to confirm that my eyes were still connected with his.

"Don't hand ya brotha over to some uppity, nigga-lovin' Yankees from the North. They just don't understand the heritage here."

I didn't respond nor reply in any way. I didn't know how to. I simply followed Sheriff back to the front of the building, ignoring the screaming newspaper reporters as I took my place in the front seat of the police car.

It was then that I met eyes with Ezra's mother. I had never formally met her, but Ezra had pointed her out to me once as he and I were walking off the makeshift baseball field near his house.

Standing next to her was Jordan, both staring at me, the pain and despair in their eyes as palpable as the humidity-thick Mississippi air.

I kept my eyes fixed on theirs as Sheriff fired the ignition and bolted the car away from the crowd.

I closed my eyes as the well of tears broke free from behind my lids and soaked my lashes and skin. I didn't say a word to Sheriff the entire way home, ignoring his superficial small talk and attempts at humor.

Once home, I raced inside, closing the door behind me as if to disconnect from the current reality. I felt my heart pulsing inside my chest, its rhythmic beating lulling me into a state of semi-calmness and composure.

I walked to the bed area, surprised to see my sister asleep in her spot, the daytime sun still beaming brightly in the window.

Exhausted, I fell beside her, aligning my body with hers, the smell of her hair soothing as I slipped into the void of darkness that waited just behind my first release of thought.

I awoke to the sound of knocking at the front door. Stumbling in the dark, I opened the door to find the faintly illuminated face of Luke Pinder, his attire reminiscent of the casual garb he had donned at the Clairmont Motel.

"Hey, Judy," he whispered, seeming to acknowledge the slumber-heavy look of my face. "Can I speak with you?"

Turning my head in the direction of a still-sleeping Francis, I nodded and closed the door behind me.

"Things are about to get pretty intense, Judy," Luke confirmed, stepping back to allow me space on the front porch. "Now that this is a criminal case, one where your brother is indicted on murder charges, you as both victim and witness, and me the prosecuting attorney, it is no longer appropriate for us to be seen or documented spending any time together outside of an official setting."

"Then why ya here, Luke?" I asked, my question seeming to stun and fluster him.

"Well, uh . . ." he choked, clearing his throat with his usual nervous, audible method. "I . . . uh. I don't know, Judy. I suppose I consider you a friend, and I just wanted to let you know why I may have to start keeping some distance. It isn't personal. It's just how these things work."

I squinted in the darkness, the fading sun barely highlighting the features of Luke's face.

"I also want you to know that I'm always here for you. No matter what. What happened to you is just so awful, and I want to be here to support you as we strive for justice in all this."

He looked up at me, his fear and uncertainty obvious in his eyes.

"I know you love your brother, Judy. And I know you don't want anything bad to happen to him. Regardless of . . ."

His voice faded as he nervously began to fidget with the lower end of his button-down shirt.

"Well, nothing has been confirmed or officially denied yet, but I think we all know where this may all be headed. I just think you're caught between a rock and a hard place. You love your brother, but you also loved Ezra."

The image of the sun behind Luke's head shadowed his face, making it a featureless sphere.

"Well, still love him, I suppose."

I shook my head.

"Luke," I sighed, the sleep in my voice still apparent, "I don't know what to think or believe anymore. On one hand, it breaks my heart that my brotha is in custody for somethin' he may or may not have done. On the other hand, someone I love is now gone. Perhaps brutally murdered. Everyone keeps tellin' me that nothin' can be confirmed without a head, but ya said his momma confirmed it was him . . . the body, so I don't know what to believe. I also don't know who it was that attacked me. All I know is I refuse to believe that the Ezra I know and love would eva' do such a thing. But if so, how can I eva' fault my brotha for goin' afta' him?"

My vision began to adjust to the soft evening light. I could see Luke's eyes, now twinkling from the front window's reflection of the pinkish-purple sky.

"I understand, Judy," he continued, still fidgeting with his shirttails. "I guess I just wanted to let you know that no matter what, I care about you."

I saw a flash of a smile ripple over his face before he nervously looked away.

"Thank ya, Luke," I stated flatly, unable to summon any form of energy or emotion in response to his words. "I agree. We need to keep our distance. Thank ya for takin' the time and makin' the effort to tell me this in person."

Luke nodded, dashing his eyes over mine before resting them back on the ground.

I watched from the kitchen window as Luke disappeared into the darkness, the sound of his throat-clearing echoing through the stillness of the night air.

I was just about to return to bed, when another knock stopped me in my tracks. Instantly, a cautious and uncertain feeling gnawed at my core. It wasn't until the second knock filled the space around me, that I ventured toward the door.

"Hey, Judy," Billy Jennings said as soon my face was visible in the small crack I made between the frame and the open door. "What did ya Yankee boyfriend have ta say?"

Sighing, I released the door, allowing it to open further on its own.

"Billy, not now," I stated. "It's been—"

Without so much as a word or gesture of warning, Billy forced the door all the way open, pushing me back with it. I started to cry out, when he cupped his cold and clammy palm over my lips.

"Ya gonna stop runnin' that smart-ass lip to me, ya hear?"

His voice cracked and simmered under the weight of his sudden anger. His breath reeked of beer and whiskey.

"Ya gonna show me the goddamn respect I'm entitled to."

I could taste his sweat as he continued to press his hand over my mouth. Several unfamiliar tastes danced over my tongue as I folded my lips in to avoid further exposure to his skin.

"People of this town revere me. They adore me. Hell, I can count six or seven females in these parts that fuckin' worship me."

With his still-free arm, he pulled my body toward him, clamping my head between his hands.

"What's wrong with ya, Judy?" he whispered into my face. "Why don't ya want me the way I want you?"

He didn't move his hand for me to respond. It was clear that he wasn't interested in any verbal reply from me. If anything, he just wanted to hear himself echo in the room around us.

"Is it 'cause ya think ya was in love with that boy?"

His breath caused my eyes to sting and water. I swear I could almost taste the alcohol that radiated from his mouth.

"Everybody's talkin' about how ya was fond of him," he continued, squeezing my head a bit tighter. "Now ya own brotha's gonna pay the price for that. When it comes to capital murda' charges in Mississippi, Judy, there're only three outcomes possible. Life in prison, death, or acquittal. The state ain't askin' for it, but the jury can most certainly hand up a death sentence if they find them boys guilty."

He shoved me, kicking my feet out from below me, forcing my body to fall to the floor with force.

"And ya brotha's guilty as sin. Everyone knows it. I'll bet he cut that poor colored kid's head off with his own bare hands."

I felt him squat down beside me in the now black chamber of the cottage.

"Too bad he didn't bring it home for ya to keep."

I started to crawl away, when Francis's voice could be heard in the shadowy distance.

"Billy?"

Immediately, Billy stood to his full height, the smell of his aftershave and liquor-heavy breath receding with him.

"Hey, Francis," he spoke in his usual cheerful voice. "I didn't realize you was here."

"What's going on?"

Suddenly, a lamp in the corner of the room lit up, Francis standing beside it.

"I was just . . . uh . . ." Billy fumbled. "I was just havin' a talk with ya sista."

Francis looked down at me, her face wavering in both sleep and confusion. It was clear she wasn't quite sure what she had heard or stumbled upon in the dark.

"Ya okay, Judy?" she asked, her brow creased and furrowed in worry.

"No," I answered immediately, slowly standing to my feet. "Billy, get the hell outta here before I call Sheriff."

I could feel Billy radiating in the slight distance between us. The rage and anger he had just exposed to me still boiled and churned beneath the corridors of his veins.

"I don't understand," I heard Francis say, her voice slowly achieving its usual tone and inflection. "Why would ya need to call Sheriff? What's going on, Judy?"

"Ya sista's just hysterical," Billy answered, turning on his heels to face me. "She's had a day of it. Everything. I can only imagine how emotionally drained she must me."

Though his words remained cheerful, caring, and buoyant, his eyes locked with mine, radiating the fire he had only just burned me with. "I just try and be sure someone is out here lookin' afta' you girls. Ya know, with Ed away and all."

He smirked at me, the same sinister look I had seen on him earlier this morning dancing over his expression again.

"Well, thank ya, Billy," Francis started. "It's very sweet and kind that—"

"Get out," I commanded, my voice loud and firm. "Just leave, Billy. We don't need ya here. We don't want ya lookin' out for us. Just go."

The rage in Billy's eyes circled his pupils and shaded his flesh.

"Now," I concluded, lifting my arm to point at the front door.

I heard Francis stumbling for a reply as Billy slowly turned from in front of me and slid his feet over the floorboards toward the door.

He smiled and nodded at Francis, peered back over his shoulder at me, and then pulled the front door shut behind him.

Francis wasted no time in getting to the bottom of what she had just witnessed.

"What happened, Judy? What was all that scufflin' and noise I heard?"

"Billy ain't who you think he is," I fired at her, my own rage and anger now bubbling to the surface of my flesh. "He was here to threaten me. He thinks we will need him to help get Ed outta this thing."

"Well, he's right," Francis said plainly, her expression as flat as the tone of her voice.

"What?" I scoffed, turning my head to face her. "No, he ain't right. We don't know if Ed is guilty or not. It's for the system to work out."

"Ed is guilty, Judy," Francis confirmed, her voice and face now echoing her usual and familiar demeanor. "Ed and the Benson boys killed that nigga the night of ya attack. They hunted him down and cut his head off like the snake he was."

I felt my body begin to convulse and shake. I struggled to catch my breath as I felt myself lower to my knees.

"Ya brotha wasted no time in protectin' ya, Judy. He wasted not one second in seekin' revenge for ya hona'."

I couldn't speak, nor could I even cry. I could only focus on my breathing, so afraid that one missed conscious effort of my lungs would keel me over in unconsciousness.

"I helped Ed bury his bloody clothes. Why do ya think ya haven't seen him in his usual work uniform the past few weeks? They was evidence. We hadta get rid of 'em."

I didn't try to stop the vomit as it popped from my mouth and onto the floor. I could only focus on my breath, counting each inhale and exhale as if my very life depended on it.

"Ya brotha committed the greatest act of love, Sista. He risked his own life to protect yours."

Tears began to intermingle with the acid around my mouth as uncontrolled sobs heaved from my chest.

"So ya better be sure ya on the right side'a all this," Francis warned, standing tall above me, peering down with an icy and judgmental glare. "Don't allow ya brotha to pay the ultimate sacrifice for ya own faults and shortcomin's."

I felt her move toward the kitchen sink, returning with a warm, wet rag.

"Don't let ya brotha pay the price for ya being a nigga-lovin' whore."

I looked up at her, tears clouding my vision and blinding the formation of any specific or familiar features.

"Now, clean ya'self," Francis seethed, tossing the wet rag onto my chest. "I'm goin' back to bed."

I fell to the floor as she shuffled off toward the bed area.

Laying my face in my own vomit, I spent the night fluctuating in and out of consciousness, tears and bile adhering to my skin and matting my hair.

As certain as the sun began to rise some hours later, so did my fear and certainty. From this day forward, nothing in my world would ever be the same. No one I loved and trusted would ever bring me comfort. And nothing I cherished and believed in would ever grant me faith again.

5

The Trial

The night before the first day of the trial, I dreamed of Ezra. We were together again on the makeshift baseball field in the colored section of town. I stood on the red clay mound, the wooden handle of a baseball bat gripped firmly within my hands. Ezra stood beside me, whispering in my ear just as the ball launched from a faceless pitcher and toward my face.

"Step over, Miss Judy-Bee," Ezra whispered confidently. "Keep ya eye on the ball and knock it outta here."

Heeding his advice, I stepped over slightly, took in a deep breath, and slammed the top of the bat against the ball just as it closed in on the space before me. With a cracking thunder, the ball zoomed over the field, the blurry players lifting their heads to watch it fly by. On the sidelines, a myriad of featureless black and white faces screamed and cheered from their vantage points. An overwhelming sense of triumph and certainty filled the air.

"Well done, Miss Judy-Bee," Ezra said, smiling. "I knew ya could do it."

"Get up," I heard Francis's voice echo, the image of Ezra's comforting and sweet face melting away.

I opened my eyes to see my sister, dressed head to toe in her finest Sunday dress. Her hair was piled high atop her head, her crimson-red lipstick practically glowing in the early morning light.

"It's time."

I struggled to awaken from my dream-state haze, watching my sister as she gracefully crossed the room toward the curtain. Pausing, she turned back, her face stern and solemn.

"I hope ya ready for this," she said in a half whisper. "The whole country has its eyes on ya."

Her words of warning jolted me to full awareness. Jumping from the bed, I quickly washed my face and brushed my hair, and hastily slid myself into my finest church dress; a dark blue number with wide, white, Pilgrim-like cuffs and collar. Sheriff and my sister stood before Sheriff's freshly washed police car as I closed the front door behind me and crossed the front porch.

"Would it have killed ya to put on a bit'a lipstick?" Francis frowned as I neared her. "Ya look like a twelve-year-old."

"Just leave her be, Francis," Sheriff scolded, opening the back door of the police cruiser for me to enter.

Francis joined Sheriff on the Ford's front bench seat, and we grumbled down the gravel pathway from the house to the red dirt road. No one spoke as we journeyed toward town, the overwhelming feeling of fear and uncertainty filling the space of the large police car like a poisonous gas. I had to keep reminding myself to breathe. I knew any focus on the impenetrable feelings of nervous terror and worry would only serve to paralyze me. My only choice was to force myself into a careless state of confidence and certainty. Revisiting my dream, I focused on the image of Ezra's smiling face as he nodded his pride and approval of my grand-slam hit with the bat. I stayed in that space until the Wayne County Courthouse filled the entire view through the windshield.

"Oh my lands," I heard Francis whisper.

Hordes of newspaper reporters and onlookers suffocated every visible space in front of the two-story brick building. The entire lawn was covered with people, all clamoring to get a closer look at the police car.

"Now, prepare ya'self, Judy," Sheriff instructed from the behind the wheel. "Every single person out there is gonna want a piece'a ya."

I felt my abdomen turn and convulse. The lack of any sustenance in my stomach was the only thing that prevented me from vomiting.

I could hear the crowd shouting my name as Sheriff exited the car and made his way to the passenger-side door. Escorting Francis to the sidewalk, he turned back to the car and reached for the rear driver's-side door handle. A burst of energy crashed over me as I took Sheriff's hand and stood to my feet. An audible gasp could be heard as people inched their eyes over every single detail of my entire being. Dozens of flashbulbs popped and hissed as I followed Sheriff to where Francis stood waiting. My sister walked beside me, the two of us marching in unison behind Sheriff toward the large, white double doors of the courthouse.

"Stay strong, Judy!" a woman shouted as I passed her. "The Lord is with ya!"

I looked up to see an endless sea of white faces. I caught a glimpse of the gathered colored group as we ascended the front steps of the courthouse, Ezra's mother, and brother, Jordan, standing front and center.

A waft of hot, stale hair inched over my entire body the moment Sheriff opened one of the giant wooden double doors. Whispers and gasps from the capacity-filled courtroom filled the air as we entered. My eyes were drawn to a vacant back section of seats, a hastily written "colored section" paper sign pinned to the edge of one of the rows.

It wasn't until Francis and I were seated that I saw my brother, Ed, his hair disheveled, his face pulled into an exhausted pinch of fear and worry. This was the first I had seen him since the arrest. I wasn't able to visit him at the jailhouse due to my position as both victim and witness in the case, not to mention the fevered interest of the national media, who would have most certainly twisted and assumed my intentions for visiting my brother into whatever motive best served their latest narrative, a narrative that seemed to alter and change nearly every hour depending on the publication and current mood of the public. One moment I was the naive, innocent victim of an aggressive Negro attack; the next, a sinister, plotting jezebel with a murderous brother. Francis, on the other hand, went to see him nearly every day. A total of three weeks had passed since the time of Ed's arrest to the start of the trial.

"Bring in the coloreds," I heard a voice boom across the open two-story square of the courthouse. I looked up to see the Wayne County circuit judge, Robert Alden, lifelong resident of Waynesboro and frequent patron of Mamey's bar, presiding behind the massive wooden judge's bench.

My eyes scanned the room for Billy, finding him seated just two rows behind me, his smirking eyes fixed directly on me.

I saw Sheriff and his two deputies escorting in Ezra's mother and brother, as well as a dozen or so of the other colored folk I had seen gathered outside. Sheriff tapped the wooden bench with his baton, impatiently barking at the slowly shuffling group to hasten their pace. I could hear the crowd grumble and groan at the sight, several racially charged whispers and scoffs clearly audible throughout the body-heat-heavy air. I turned back toward Judge Alden, who could obviously hear the uproar, but did nothing to silence it.

"All right," the judge barked, peering over the crowd through the half-moon spectacles that rested on the lower tip of his nose. "I'd like both attorneys and all accused to stand."

The crowd fell silent as the entire front row of the room stood to their feet. Luke Pinder stood alone across from Jim Hemming, the defense attorney, Ron and Fred Benson, and Ed. Unlike the Benson brothers, who stood confidently with wry, half smiles locked over their faces, Ed stood hunched and defeated, almost as if he had already been convicted and was just awaiting his sentence.

"Now, I will not allow my courtroom to become some sorta spectacle," Judge Alden announced. "I know there is an awful lot of press attention on all this, far more than I think is necessary, but that does not mean I will allow some form of external influence to sway or dictate the law as I see fit. I will not tolerate some highfalutin showin' off, nor will I tolerate mere laziness and unpreparedness. This is a court a'law, my court a'law, and it shall be respected as such."

The judge moved his eyes over the entire first row, paying special attention to Luke.

"This is not a circus, and I will not tolerate any sorta games."

The room stood still. Only the sound of the countless overhead ceiling fans could be heard squeaking in their labor.

"Do I make myself perfectly clear, gentlemen?"

"Yes, Your Honor," the row of men replied as one.

"Very well," Judge Alden nodded, signaling his approval. "Now, one more thing before you're seated."

This time, the judge allowed his eyes to tour the entirety of the courtroom.

"I'm a judge here in the great state of Mississippi. We here in the South have a heritage and a value system that dates back generations. I will not allow for more liberal opinions to fluctuate or alter the course of Southern justice."

The crowd murmured in response; the flash of camera bulbs could be heard popping and sizzling in the press balcony above.

"All right then," Judge Alden declared. "Let's get this thing goin'."

The day ended after four and a half hours. Despite the fact that it was inappropriate to do so, seeing as though it were only opening statements, most of which were presented by Luke, Jim Hemming responded with objections and outward pleas to the judge to interject or stop Luke. Most of the time, Judge Alden obliged Jim Hemming, but reluctantly allowed for Luke to carry out his obviously carefully and meticulously planned and rehearsed opening statement.

Sheriff stood beside Francis and me as his two deputies cleared the courtroom. I could feel Francis waving beside me. I looked up just in time to see Ed turn his head, a smile now gracing his lips. When I turned my head forward again, I locked eyes with Ezra's mother. She was standing guard at the edge of the colored section, where the group waited patiently for the deputies to return to release them.

Shamefully, I hung my head, the piercing intensity of her eyes burning into the top of my scalp.

The same crowd greeted us as Sheriff escorted Francis and me back to his police car.

Several shouts of "may God be with ya" and "God bless ya" filled the air as we inched down the single pathway toward the street.

After Sheriff had secured me behind the rear driver's-side door of the police cruiser, I again connected eyes with Ezra's mother just as she was descending the steps of the courthouse. Dutifully following the two deputies, her eyes were locked on mine, her attention oblivious to the angry and racially charged slurs that were shouted her way by various members of the gathered all-white group of gawking onlookers. Though I wanted to look away, I couldn't. I met her eyes with my own as Sheriff loaded Francis into the front seat of the cruiser and rushed over to the driver's side.

No one spoke until we were nearly home.

"Ya both did a fine job today, ladies," Sheriff commented, smiling at me through the rearview mirror. "It's not easy just sittin' there all quiet and all while that Yankee boy bops around runnin' his mouth. Good thing ol' Judge Alden is keepin' such a short chain on him."

I looked to Francis, who kept her gaze fixed dreamily out the front passenger-side window.

"I don't think y'all gonna haveta worry too much about ya brotha, Ed," Sheriff continued. "From the way things went today, Jim Hemming is gonna bring this thing home safe and sound."

Neither Francis nor I said goodbye to Sheriff as he opened our car doors and escorted us up the front porch steps of our house. He confirmed the time he would pick us up in the morning, then quietly returned to his still-running police vehicle.

Francis didn't speak to me for the rest of the night. We ate our dinner in separate silences at different times. I waited for her to fall asleep before entering the bedroom area, too afraid and uncomfortable that she would want to start another argument or altercation. Thankfully, I found her silent and sleeping instead. Without a sound, I slid my body beside her beneath the covers, an ongoing ritual I had been faithful to my entire life.

The attorneys wasted no time in utilizing and exhausting their limited set of witnesses. For three days straight, Ezra's brother, Jordan, and two other colored boys were interrogated by both the defense and prosecution. Where Luke Pinder gently questioned and encouraged them, Jim Hemming hollered, screamed, and terrorized them. Judge Alden did nothing to stop nor temper this. Instead, he let

Jim rant and rave like a madman, angrily accusing the three colored boys of bias and prejudice against the white men.

"Is it not true that ya have a personal hatred toward all white men?" Jim bellowed over the echo of the courtroom. "Isn't it true ya'd willingly accuse any white man of murda' just to see him suffa'?"

The boys struggled to stand firm in their claims, despite the unprofessional and venomous haze Jim Hemming painted over the courtroom.

It was on the fourth day that Ezra's mother, Berta Washington, was called to the witness stand.

Luke gently guided her through the retelling of the process which had allowed her to identify the remains of her son.

"I just knew it was him," she declared, her eyes fixed straight on Luke's. "I could feel it in my bones. A momma always knows."

"Objection, Ya Hona'," Jim Hemming cried. "Are we gonna allow a woman's talk of feelin's and intuition to identify a body with certainty? This ain't evidence. This's just panderin' to the jury."

"Sustained," Judge Alden agreed. "The jury is asked to ignore the witness's statement."

I looked over at the jury, a collection of Waynesboro's hodgepodge of similar-looking white men, various ages and hair color, or lack thereof, similar Sunday church-wear, some with glasses and some without, yet all male, and all white. The twelve jurors nodded in unison, some smirking and scoffing at Ms. Washington.

"Mr. Pinder, only the coroner's report will be allowed as evidence regarding the identity of the body," Judge Alden continued. "We have Wayne County coroner Martin Geralds here in the audience if ya'd like to add him to the witness list."

"No, Your Honor," Luke sighed. "Mr. Geralds makes it abundantly clear in his, well, what I consider to be a haphazard, erroneous report, that the body could not be accurately identified without a head."

In what appeared to be a moment of sheer rage and defiance, Luke turned his head toward Ed and the Benson brothers.

"Where's the head, boys!" he screamed. "What'd you do with this poor boy's head! This grieving mother, where is her son's head!"

"Order!" Judge Alden shouted at the top of his lungs. "How dare ya make a mockery of my courtroom, Mr. Pinder! Another stunt like that and I will hold ya in contempt! Now, finish with ya witness and then sit down!"

Luke nodded, mumbling something under his breath just loud enough for the courtroom to overhear.

"What was that, Mr. Pinder?" the judge yelled. "Do you have somethin' ya'd like to add to this? I'll be more than happy to quote ya in my contempt order."

"I apologize, Your Honor. I have no further questions for Ms. Washington."

"Fine," Judge Alden said, his face now a peachy pink of blood-pressure-raised anger. "Mr. Hemming, you may address the witness."

I couldn't bear to watch as Jim Hemming wasted no time in reducing Berta Washington to tears.

"Isn't it true that ya son had a habit of disobeyin' county curfew orders? I have several statements from Sheriff Roberts and his deputies claimin' they had to escort ya son back to the Negro section of town afta' dark on far more than one occasion, specifically from the road that leads to and from the home of Judith Bracewell. How then does that help in the argument that Ezra Washington was not in the area the night Judith Bracewell was brutally attacked and raped? Given his habit of curfew disobedience, I'd wager to say he was most certainly in the area."

"Objection, Your Honor!" Luke cried. "The defense is presenting speculation. I ask that it be struck from the record. Immediately!"

Judge Alden glared over his spectacles at Luke, a rage and fire spinning vibrantly in his eyes.

"Oh, immediately, Mr. Pinder? Is that so?"

The crowd stopped moving about in their bench seats. A pin could be heard tapping the ground as the entire room hushed and silenced into a breathless, anticipating mass.

"If ya think ya gonna somehow try and persuade or intimidate me with ya highfalutin' Boston law degree, ya can think again, good sir. I'm the law around here, Mr. Pinder, and I'll be damned if some loud-mouthed, uppity Yankee boy from the North is gonna come into my courtroom and bark orders at me!"

"Your Honor, I didn't mean to—"

"Quiet!" the judge interrupted the remorsefully pleading Luke. "I will not warn ya again!"

Luke nodded and returned to his chair.

"Now, I will allow this strike from the record. Gentleman of the jury, please ignore Mr. Hemming's last statement to the witness. I will not allow any insinuatin', Mr. Hemming."

"Yes, Ya Hona'," Jim Hemming agreed, nodding his head apologetically at the judge.

"Now, ya may continue."

The next half hour consisted of Jim Hemming annihilating Ms. Washington in a more crass and cunning way, which seemed to appease the judge and not disturb the prosecution. The sole team member of Mr. Pinder sat with his head facing down, nervously shuffling through paperwork while Jim Hemming went to town discrediting not only Ms. Washington's son, but also the witness herself.

"Isn't it true that you were once caught lyin' to Sheriff Roberts some three years or so back?" Jim boomed over the room. "Hmm?"

Ms. Washington slowly nodded her head, her eyes locked on Jim Hemming's.

"Ya need to speak up, hon, so ya response can go on record."

"Yes," Ms. Washington quietly confirmed, keeping her eyes fixed firmly over Jim's.

"Uh, yes, what?" Jim replied.

Without a sigh or so much as a blink, Ms. Washington followed up her answer with a boisterous and lively, "Yes sir!"

The courtroom began to shuffle and murmur, the apparent audacity of her answer causing an unseen source of anger and tension to blanket the room. I looked toward the jury, where all twelve men scoffed and shook their heads disapprovingly.

Jim blasted Ms. Washington for another twenty minutes, ragefully forcing her to detail a time when she had told Sheriff she had not seen her departed husband's brother, her brother-in-law, after he had been accused of stealing trash from Norman Goody's farm dustbin. Ms. Washington had denied seeing him that day, though Sheriff and his deputies had later found the man hiding out behind Ms. Washington's small wood-framed house. The account jogged my memory to the graphic aftermath. Closing my eyes, I could clearly remember seeing Sheriff publicly whip Ms. Washington's brother-in-law in the center of Main Street. I was able to witness the entire awful event from behind the front glass of Dolsan's Grocery.

After satiating his need to color Ms. Washington as not only a weak and discreditable witness, but also as a bold-faced liar, who had not only lied to local law enforcement, but also openly and willingly harbored a sought-after perpetrator, Jim Hemming concluded his line of questioning and took his seat.

It was clear the direction the trial was taking as the courtroom cleared out later that evening.

"They need to just let them boys go home tonight," I heard a woman say as she moved to join the slow-moving march of the crowd. "It's a damn shame to keep those po' boys all locked up like that when there ain't no proof they did a damn thing."

I didn't make eye contact with any of the onlookers who shouted religious-laced comments at me, nor did I bat an eye as the same gaggle of reporters vied for my attention. Without a sound, I dropped myself into the backseat of Sheriff's cruiser, now a nightly ritual, and blankly allowed my gaze to venture out over the distance beyond the car door window. Again, my eyes met with Ms. Washington's as she followed one of Sheriff's deputies from the courthouse, her face sullen, her eyes wide. I felt an overwhelming feeling of grief and loss wash over me. The image of her face haunted me as we drove through the rain-soaked mud paths toward home. The memory of her eyes lingered behind my lids as I closed them for slumber, only to find her even in my dreams, haunting, staring.

The prosecution called me to the witness stand the next day. The crowd fell completely silent as I made my way to the front of the courtroom. I could feel every single pair of eyes following my every step as I inched toward the witness seat. I made eye contact with Ed, his eyes swollen and red, large dark bags circling under each socket. I could feel my heart pulsing in my ears, the thundering drum of each beat deafening.

"First off, Ms. Bracewell," Luke began, gently smiling and nodding at me as he neared the witness stand, "the state of Mississippi would like to thank you for your courage and bravery in agreeing to testify. What happened to you is an absolute tragedy, and I would suffice it to say that everyone present in this courtroom today not only harbors deep sadness and sympathy for you, but also commends and admires your commitment to seeking justice in this matter."

I nodded, swallowing so loudly I just knew even the reporters in the rear second-floor balcony could hear it.

"I would like to kindly remind the gentlemen of the jury that the crime which was committed against Ms. Bracewell is not why we are here today. This is not a rape trial, but a murder trial. The gentlemen indicted on these murder charges sit before you today."

The heads of the jury turned in unison as Luke gestured toward Ed and the Benson brothers.

"The question we must answer here is whether or not these men committed the act of murder against a young Ezra Washington. It is not Ezra's sins or alleged crimes that are on trial today but the cause of his death and who is responsible for it."

I could see Fred and Ron Benson smirking in the corner of my eye. Ed lowered his head to his chest.

"Now, Ms. Bracewell, please recount for the jury, to the best of your memory, what it was that happened to you on the night of the unfortunate assault."

After several warbled attempts at forming a set of cohesive words, I was finally able to slowly relive the memory of the hazy, rainy night to the echo of the capacity-filled courtroom. The room was so still and silent one could swear the collection of human heartbeats could be heard in a single, unified pulse. Finally, I concluded my account to the satisfaction of Luke's coaxing questions, many of them focused on Ezra's and my secret relationship. It was obvious he was only interested in establishing the possibility that it was indeed Ezra who had attacked me, which would have provided a clear and concise motive for Ed and the Benson boys to murder him.

I struggled to swallow a mouthful of room-temperature water as Jim Hemming made his approach to the witness stand.

"The defense would like to echo Mr. Pinder's sentiments regardin' ya most unfortunate sufferin'," Jim began, gently placing a hand over mine. "Mr. Pinder is also correct in pointin' out that what happened to ya, dear, sweet girl, is not the focus of this trial. It should be though, as similar crimes such as this have gone on for far too long in this great state and all across this nation, often unreported and unprosecuted."

Jim spun dramatically on his heels to face the entire courtroom.

"Ladies and gentlemen, it does my defense case not a bit a' good to vilify or demonize Ezra Washington. In fact, it does just the opposite. For me to carry on, confirming the evidence that it was indeed Mr. Washington who animalistically attacked and raped Judith Bracewell, only serves to condemn the men I am defendin'. It paints the picture for a clear and understood motive."

Judge Alden tapped his gavel as the room erupted into a collection of murmurs and gasps.

"But I will continue by also remindin' the fine gentlemen of the jury that it is the prosecution's job to prove their case to ya beyond a shadow of a doubt. No matter how hard my new friend and esteemed colleague of the law tries, this simply cannot be done."

Jim flashed a sly smile at Luke as he continued to speak.

"No, gentlemen, it is impossible, for unless someone is able to provide further evidence that the headless corpse pulled from the muck is indeed the mortal remains of Ezra Washington, then there is no case here. How can these fine men of our community have murdered a man who is still missin'? For all we know, Ezra Washington is still on the run, guilty and ravenous in his dangerous ways, free to brutally attack and rape more innocent white women who have the misfortune of crossin' his path."

I looked to Luke, who only looked away the moment he caught my gaze.

"No, gentlemen. We are wastin' the court's fine time here by conductin' a murda' trial for a case that has a still-unidentified body as its key evidence."

Jim Hemming walked to his place at the defense table.

"In my hand, gentlemen of the jury," he said, sweeping a folder from the giant wood surface of the table, "is the official coroner's report. And despite Mr. Pinder's opinion that it is erroneous and flawed, there is simply no way possible for there to be an absolute positive identification of this body."

Jim closed in on the jury box, shaking his head as he moved.

"This ain't no science-fiction picture, folks," Jim announced, shaking the coroner's report in his hand. "Without a head, there ain't no way for anyone to accurately and definitely identify this body. Sure, we have fingers, but there ain't no fingerprint record for Ezra Washington, nor was there any fingerprints left at the crime scene."

Jim turned his head to look at me, smiling as he nodded.

"This poor, innocent young woman is the crime scene."

I could feel the sympathy and pity of the entire room drape over me like a heavy blanket. Without hesitation, I lowered my head in shame.

"So again, the fact of the matta' remains. Is the body discovered in a Wayne County creek the body of Ezra Washington? For only with certainty that it is can we proceed with a relevant murda' trial. Until then, gentlemen, ya have no other choice but to acquit these men."

I raised my head just in time to see Ed peering up at me, his head still hung.

"I have no furtha' questions for the witness, Ya Hona'."

I wasn't looking when I heard Ed's voice, but I lifted my head again just in time to see him stand from his chair.

"I did it, Ya Hona'," he said, his voice strong and clear.

The entire courtroom gasped in one massive, collective sweep of air.

"Wha—" Judge Alden cleared his throat. "Son, I think ya need to consult with ya counsela'. I'll strike this outburst from—"

"I know where the boy's head is," Ed continued, his voice now shaking. "I can lead ya to it. Please, listen to what I'm tellin' ya."

The entire courtroom erupted in sound. My eyes locked onto Ed, my entire body trembling. Tears burst from my eyes as I watched Jim Hemming scramble toward Ed.

"Court adjourned until furtha' notice," Judge Alden finally declared. "Sheriff, clear this courtroom."

I sat in a stunned, tearful silence as Sheriff and his two deputies struggled to usher the aghast, chattering crowd toward the double doors of the courthouse. Jim Hemming hovered in front of Ed, but Berta Washington was clearly visible to me as she remained seated in the colored section of the courtroom audience. Several others surrounded her, including Jordan, all visibly attempting to provide some form of comfort. Ms. Washington stared straight ahead though, unmoved and unaware of her concerned bystanders. Her face remained poised and stoic, a thick stream of tears flooding her skin.

It was only when Luke Pinder approached me that I broke from my sudden paralysis. I couldn't make out the words he spoke as he pulled me from the witness stand and forced me at Sheriff. My eyes remained fixed on Ms. Washington as Sheriff led me toward the front of the courthouse, her eyes finally locking with mine just moments before Sheriff pulled me from the building.

The crowd was wild. Onlookers, the courtroom audience, and the reporters were all shouting and screaming over one another. No one seemed to notice as Sheriff quickly led me toward his parked police car.

I heard Sheriff yell for one of his deputies as he slammed the car door shut beside me, instructing the man to drive me home. I turned my head to see Francis at the top of the courtroom steps, her eyes wide, her face frozen. She didn't blink nor signal for my attention. She only stared, my imagination assuming the sound of her heavy-beating heart as she blankly surveyed the scene before her.

The car ride home was a silent haze, though I could sort of hear the muffled sound of the deputy as he nervously filled the space with pointless chatter.

The deputy stayed outside the cottage while I ventured inside. A deafening ring in my ears brought me to my knees, my stomach in knots, my tears reinvigorating as I began to retch.

I was in the same position a few hours later when Sheriff arrived with Francis.

"You girls stay in this house, ya hear?" he shouted, pointing at each of us before slamming the front door.

I looked at Francis, her face still as blank and vacant as it had been on the courthouse steps.

Francis eventually moved to the kitchen table, but did not speak. I remained on the floor, my retching continuing, but my body unable to provide any substance.

I wasn't sure how much time had passed when Sheriff finally returned, but I imagined it had been hours. Francis was asleep at the table, her head slumped over her arms in a hair-disheveled heap. I was still awake on the floor, my mind drifting in and out of conscious awareness.

"Get off the floor, Judy," I heard Sheriff say as he entered the cottage. "Francis, honey, wake up."

I felt Sheriff clasp his arm under mine, lifting me with ease. I stumbled as he led me to the kitchen table. Francis was just lifting her head as Sheriff sat me in the chair next to her.

"Listen," Sheriff commanded as he took the seat across from us, "they found the head."

Francis and I remained still; silent and unflinching.

"It was exactly where Ed said it was, a mile or so in the woods behind the Benson property."

Sheriff fidgeted with his shirt-secured badge for a long moment before continuing.

"Now, I don't know what all this means regardin' the case. I guess we'll just haveta wait and see what the judge decides tomorrow. For now though, girls, things certainly ain't lookin' very good for ya brotha."

Sheriff moved his eyes over mine.

"Judy," he spoke softly, "how ya holdin' up, baby girl?"

I gave a slight nod, though I felt fresh tears invading the front of my face.

"Y'all just gonna haveta stay here for now," Sheriff continued, moving his hands across the table toward us. "I'll return sometime tomorrow after court. It's best that ya both stay away from all this for the time bein'."

I watched as Sheriff placed one hand over mine, the other over Francis's.

"You girls should try and get some rest. Deputy Johnson will stay here with ya till mornin'."

Neither Francis nor I moved from the table after Sheriff left. We simply sat in silence, the deafening drumming of our collective heartbeats lulling us into individual bouts of restless sleep.

It was nearly dusk when Sheriff finally arrived the next day. Francis had long gone to bed, never uttering a word to me the few times she moved for water or to use the toilet. I, on the other hand, never moved from the table. The echo of Ed's voice, the tearful stare of Ms. Washington's face, the pelt of the cold rain that had slapped my skin the night of the attack—it all swirled within my brain in an infinite whirl. It wasn't until Sheriff began to speak, that I broke from the trance and realized the passing of time.

"Where's Francis?" he asked, darting his eyes around the room.

"Bed," I croaked, my voice raw and dry in its first summoned use in more than a day.

Sheriff returned a few moments later, a sleep-weary Francis clutched to his arm.

"The judge declared a mistrial," he announced, gently assisting Francis into a chair.

I shook my head in confusion.

"Do ya understand what that means?" Sheriff asked, his eyes bouncing between Francis's and mine.

I shook my head again.

"It means this whole thing is about to start ova'. If ya brotha pleads guilty, then there won't be anotha' trial, only a sentencin'. His best hope now is for a plea bargain that will result in a life sentence ratha' than the death penalty. The gas chamba' is certainly a possible outcome with a guilty conviction by a jury, 'specially with the head now in evidence."

My brain raced to try to compute what Sheriff was saying.

"It means ya brotha is more than likely gonna spend the rest of his life in prison for this."

Francis began to cry, while I could only shake my head. I hardly noticed when my subconscious mind turned my head so I could vomit. A wet, clear blob of saliva and some form of stomach fluid dropped to the floor beside me.

"I'm keepin' Deputy Johnson here for the time bein'. I'm sure some a'those money-hungry newspapa' reporta's are gonna be headin' over here to get at ya, Judy."

Sheriff moved to the sink to fetch a rag. Gently and carefully, he wiped my face before squatting to his knees to clean the floor, the popping of his joints echoing like dry tree branches.

"Y'all make a list of whateva' it is you need food-wise and all, and I'll be sure to have it sent ova'."

Sheriff moved back to the sink, rinsed out the rag, and returned to the tableside.

"Don't neitha' one of ya dare venture from this house," he commanded. "Until I have a betta' grip on what's going on, I want ya both to stay put."

I kept my eyes on the floor as I heard Sheriff shuffle toward the front door.

"Comfort each otha'," he concluded as he twisted the doorknob, inviting in the thick, humidity-choked air of the Mississippi night. "You two may be all that's left of this family."

Sheriff closed the door gently behind him. In the distance, I could hear him rev his patrol car and accelerate into the night. I peered out the window at Deputy Johnson, who was napping in his squad car. Switching off every light, I carefully and silently led my sister toward the bed area. Tucking her in, I moved to the window, my last visible memory that of the moon as it sailed with the stars above the nearby tree line.

I awoke to the sound of shuffling on the front porch. It had been two whole days since we last saw Sheriff. As promised, he had sent a parcel of food and supplies to hold us over for at least a week. The two deputies exchanged duties as watchdog, though, to my knowledge, no reporters ever tried to access the house.

Francis remained asleep as I crept from the bed and toward the front window. In the shadows of near midnight, I could see Sheriff's large Ford police car, Billy Jennings's granny's maroon 1950 Ford Coupe parked just behind it.

"Get on home, Randy. I got it from here," I heard Sheriff tell the deputy, who sleepily stumbled off the front porch and toward his waiting squad car. Within seconds, Sheriff was in the house, a dark figure close behind him.

Nervous, I tiptoed into the living room area just as Sheriff switched on the room's sole table lamp. Immediately, the face of Mississippi attorney general Richard Jennings, Billy's father, appeared from the darkness.

"Don't be scared, Judy," Sheriff said softly, moving to my side. "Just have a seat."

I didn't take my eyes off Mr. Jennings as I felt Sheriff lower me into a seated position on the worn velvet sofa. Mr. Jennings sat across from me, filling Ed's faded brown easy chair like a king on a throne.

"Hey, Judy," he smiled, his brilliant-white teeth glowing in the dim light of the room. "How are ya, honey?"

I shook my head, fumbling for words.

"I need to speak with ya, sweetheart. It's a very serious matta'."

I watched as the state attorney general nodded at Sheriff, who returned the nod, made one final glance at me, and then exited the cottage. No one said a word about Francis, who I assumed was still sleeping behind the draped curtain on the far side of the living area.

"As ya know, Judge Alden declared a mistrial," Mr. Jennings began, moving his eyes over mine. "Do ya understand what that means, Judy?"

I nodded, too nervous to speak.

"It means you could lose ya brotha foreva'."

The attorney general's words pierced into my ears like tiny bee stings. I flinched at the imagined pain.

"Now, there may be somethin' we can do."

I lifted my eyes, Mr. Jennings's glare piercing the space between us.

"My son," he continued, the hazy image of Billy Jennings's face stumbling into my brain, "he's completely in love with ya."

I felt my brow furrow as Mr. Jennings continued to speak, detailing his only son's passionate affection for me.

"Now, I see ya as a fine young woman, Judy, don't get me wrong. But for me personally, the situation with you and the young Negro boy has a bit too much unsavory flava' for my taste buds. Still, my son is unmovin' in his decree."

The words that filled the room were suddenly so alien and dreamlike. I felt myself pinch the skin of my forearm in an attempt to ensure consciousness.

"Ya brotha's a fool for takin' the blame on all this," Mr. Jennings continued. "The DA sent Pinder here 'cause he knew this case stood no chance'a winnin'. Havin' Pinder prosecutin' just made us all look good given his background in civil rights matta's and whatnot. Still, with no head on that body, there was no way there was eva' gonna be any murder convictions. Now, though, with ya brotha leadin' 'em to the head and all, if he sticks by his confession and pleads guilty, he's gonna get life for sure. They may plea bargain for life with the possibility of parole if he agrees to testify against the Bensons in a retrial. Otherwise, Judy, ya brotha has most certainly done himself in."

Mr. Jennings paused.

"Ya got any whiskey?" he asked, turning his head toward the kitchen.

I blinked rapidly, unsure how to respond.

"Ah, never mind. I gotta drive right back to Jackson afta' this. Just a glass a' wata' will do."

Mr. Jennings waited in silence until I returned from the kitchen with a glass of tap water.

I returned to my place on the sofa while he loudly gulped the liquid down, letting out a dramatic and audible sigh of satisfaction upon concluding every drop.

"Thank ya, dear," he said, nodding. "Doctor says I gotta keep these ol' kidneys hydrated."

He placed the now empty glass on the small table beside him, bumping the lamp enough to where it shook the entire visible lighting in the room.

"Now," he continued, clearing his throat, "I'd just rather let the whole thing be and allow for ya brotha to face justice however the next judge sees fit, be it a sentencin' or a retrial, but it seems my son feels the need to intervene."

I felt my head cock in confusion, my face still matted in several coats of disbelief.

"If you can convince ya brotha to not try and be some kind of martyr for Negro justice," he stated, ensuring that my eyes were locked with his, "I can arrange for him to disappear."

He waited for a moment as his words fell upon my ears. I could only imagine the look of sheer and utter shock and disbelief that had to be gripping my expression.

"If ya agree to marry my son," he stated matter-of-factly, "I can save ya brotha's life."

I laughed. I wasn't sure if it were instinctual, emotional, or sheer coincidence, but I laughed. Mr. Jennings's face twitched in confusion.

"What is it?" he asked.

"Marry ya son?" I questioned, my voice hoarse and dry. "Why would I just up and marry ya son?"

The state's most powerful man of the law gaped at me in complete shock.

"Because my son is Billy Jennings. My son . . . the son of the state attorney general. Elie Jennings's grandson. Are ya . . . ?"

He shook his head in disbelief.

"Are ya serious, girl? Marryin' into my family is the absolute best thing that could eva' happen to ya."

He moved his eyes slowly over my face, a twist of judgment now gripping his expression.

"Ya damaged goods now, honey," he spoke plainly. "Not only will no man want ya because you was raped, but ain't no man livin' willin' to suffer the shame of the entire world knowin' his bride was fucked by some nigga."

A fire reminiscent of the one I had seen in Billy's eyes twisted and circled behind Mr. Jennings's glare.

"As I said, I do not approve of this union, but it is not for me to decide. If my son is ready and willin' to deal with ya shame, then so be it."

He sat back in the easy chair, his eyes never moving off mine.

"Sure, I could stand my ground and refuse this marriage, but I'm no fool. I know the price for that is losin' my son."

He leaned forward, inching his face closer to mine.

"I'd rather have the town gossip and rumor about my new daughter-in-law's nigga-lovin' ways than risk the chance of neva' speakin' with my son again."

"I . . ." I started, but my voice gave out.

"Convince Ed to leave, Judy," Mr. Jennings repeated, standing to his feet. "If he stays, they gonna make sure he lives out the rest'a his days locked away at Mississippi State Penitentiary."

I watched as the head of the most powerful family in Wayne County inched toward the front door of our quaint cottage.

"The choice is yours."

He didn't wait for a response as he pulled open the door, revealing a waiting Sheriff. I could hear the two men exchange a few words before Sheriff reentered the room, gently closing the door behind him.

"Get dressed, Judy," he instructed. "Mr. Jennings wants me to take ya down to the jailhouse."

"But . . ." I started again, but my voice failing me once more.

"Hey," Sheriff said in a loud whisper, moving quickly to the sofa, "as far as I can see, honey, ya ain't gotta choice in this. Ya can't sit here and tell me ya ain't gonna take up this offa'. Ya can't sit there and tell me ya just gonna be selfish and allow ya brotha to be handed over to spend the rest'a his life behind bars."

A well of fear and uncertainty glazed over my skin with the oozing of fresh tears.

"They shippin' Ed off to Meridian in the mornin'," Sheriff whispered. "Now is the only chance we have for ya to see him."

My tears quickened their pace, my breath losing its rhythm to the impulse of sudden sobbing.

"Get up, Judy!" Sheriff commanded in a louder whisper. "I ain't gonna sit here and allow ya brotha to go down for protectin' his sista."

I flinched as Sheriff forcefully grabbed my arm and pulled me from the couch. I continued to sob as he pushed me behind the bedroom curtain, a sleeping Francis illuminated in the moonlight from the small window.

"Ya think it's right for ya brotha to pay with his life for protec-tin' his sista?" Sheriff continued to chastise from behind the curtain. "He might be feelin' guilty now, but in the long run, he does not deserve to lose his freedom for this. No nigga's life is as important as a white man's. I don't care what the circumstances are. That's just how it is."

Francis, now awake, furrowed her brow and lifted her head as I fumbled through the dresser for something to wear. Tears clouded my eyes as my heaving chest continued to succumb to the weight of my relentless sobbing.

"This whole thing is the very hand of God at work if ya ask me. Here it is, the wealthiest family in the county has a son that is not only willin' to overlook ya sins and transgressions, but is willin' to save ya brotha in the process. With Ed gone, eitha' through the arrangements Mr. Jennings is offerin' or to the hands of the justice system, you two girls will be alone. Marryin' Billy ensures ya both will be taken care of."

Anticipating further lecturing, I tossed on a pair of old work slacks and one of Ed's dirty nightshirts. Francis and I met eyes just before I moved behind the curtain, her face confused yet sturdy.

Sheriff nodded at Mr. Jennings, who was waiting behind the wheel of his mother's Ford Coupe. He nodded back, fired up the car, and peeled off into the darkness.

I fell into the passenger side of Sheriff's car, my breathing now completely overpowered by my sobbing. It didn't take Sheriff long to chastise me for it.

"Ya stop that cryin', girl," he commanded. "What Mr. Jennings said was true. Ain't no man gonna want ya now that ya been violated, much less at the hands of some rabid nigga."

Confirming that he had eavesdropped from the front door, Sheriff continued to echo Mr. Jennings's stern words of warning regarding the supposed inevitable outcome of my brother's fate if I chose to decline the offer. I could only cry, never uttering a single word during the entire car ride to the jailhouse.

"Pull ya'self together now, Judy," Sheriff urged, snatching a handkerchief from his front shirt pocket and dabbing my face.

"Hey . . ."

He lifted my chin with his index finger.

"Rememba' what I told ya?" he said, locking his eyes over mine in the faint light from the single bulb that hung beside the doorway to the jail. "Ya hona' ya race. Ya stick by ya blood."

He didn't wait for me to reply as he exited the car and made his way to the passenger-side door.

Fearing further scolding, I exited the vehicle, the dark yellow light from the jailhouse entrance pulling my gaze.

I could feel my heartbeat in the roof of my mouth and beneath each tooth as I followed Sheriff into the Wayne County Jailhouse.

"Wait here," Sheriff instructed once we were safely inside the building. It was several minutes before he returned. "Come."

I followed him into a windowless room, a wide-eyed Ed shackled and bound in the corner.

"Judy," he whispered, causing me to lose my breath.

"Go on, Judy," Sheriff directed, nodding toward Ed before exiting the room and closing the door.

"Why . . . what . . ." Ed murmured.

"Shh," I shook my head, shuffling in a tearful stumble to embrace my brother.

I could feel Ed sobbing as he rested his head on my shoulder, his shackled arms unable to embrace me back.

We stood silently for what seemed like hours, our skin touching for the first time in weeks.

"Why ya here?" he whispered, keeping his head on my shoulder.

"I need ya to do somethin' for me," I whispered back, surprised at how solid and sturdy my words were.

"Okay, Judy. Ya know I'd do anything for my baby sista."

"No, Ed," I raised my voice to speaking level. "This is the most serious thing I will eva' ask of ya."

Ed lifted his head, his eyes drifting over mine curiously.

"I need ya to agree to go with whateva' Billy's daddy offa's ya."

Ed's brow furrowed in confusion.

"He can arrange for ya to disappear. I don't know to where or with who, but I just know it'll be safe."

"Judy, no," Ed stated. "I need to pay the price for what I've done. I need—"

"Stop!" I shouted, my voice echoing around the small room like a sudden gunshot. "Ya don't have a choice, Ed. You'll do this for me. Just go. Don't ask any questions. Please, do this for me. Do this for Francis."

"But, Sis, I don't under—"

"Just go, Ed. Whateva' it is. Just go."

I started sobbing again, the weight of my tears dropping me to my knees.

"Okay," he whispered, lowering himself beside me. "I don't understand, but if ya this serious . . . I . . . ."

I lifted my face, Ed's tear-stained gaze just inches from mine.

"I'm so sorry, Judy," he sobbed, "for all this. I just wanted to protect ya. I never meant to hurt ya. I swear it."

"I know, Ed," I sobbed. "I know. That's why ya haveta do this for me. I can't let ya spend ya life in prison. I can't lose ya too. Daddy, Momma, Ezra . . . I just can't, Ed. I can't lose ya."

Ed fell into my arms, the two of us pinched and restricted by his cumbersome shackles.

"Okay," he whispered in agreement. "I understand."

I held my brother for what felt like an eternity but passed in mere seconds. Ed never questioned the details, and I didn't speak a word to him regarding my side of the agreement with Mr. Jennings. Instead, we relived old times: memories of Daddy, Momma, and Francis. Ed recounted the tale of his favorite Christmas, a story I had heard a dozen or more times before. It was the year I was born, and Momma and Daddy couldn't afford the electric bill after buying Ed and me our gifts, so we all had huddled together in front of the makeshift fireplace Daddy had constructed in the kitchen.

The sun was just peeking over the treetops as Sheriff led me from the jailhouse. The taste of Ed's tear-soaked cheek lingered over my lips as we drove back toward the cottage, neither Sheriff nor I speaking a single word.

I collapsed over the threshold once we finally made it back. My last half-conscious memory was that of Sheriff and Frances carrying my limp body to the bed. I could still taste Ed's tears as I drifted into the blackness.

Part II

Jackson, Mississippi
1962

6

The Letters

His hair was golden blond, the color of sunflowers glowing in the autumn sun. His eyes, the blue of untouched pools, their clarity and brilliance rivaling that of the diamond ring effect of a total solar eclipse. His laughter lingered in the air around him, his boyish voice canceling out all other rival sounds in the space he dwelled in.

William Johnson Jennings Jr., my son, my soul's greatest pride and joy, bounced along the gravel pathway that led to the swing set, a tow of a dozen or so other similar-aged children following his lead. It was my son's birthday, his fifth to be exact; he was conceived with Billy Jennings just weeks after we were married.

Billy and I had a spectacular wedding. Nearly every resident of Wayne County was in attendance. Much of the national press covered the event, the town prince marrying the poor rape victim of a murdered Negro a sensational front-page headline across the country. Francis had been my maid of honor, a role she relished and reveled in like a star on the Broadway stage. To those observant, it was clear that my sister was far more celebratory and enthusiastic about my wedding than I was; me, the bride. My clouded, hazy memories of that day remain distant yet lingering. I can only recall weeping beforehand, my face red and puffy as I marched solo down the regal aisle of Waynesboro Methodist. Thankfully, the tearstained crimson of my face did not register in the black-and-white photographs, both those in the papers and those produced by the wedding photographer. My heart was heavy on that day, lost in heartache over Ezra and Ed.

Five years on and I still had no idea where my only brother was. Mr. Jennings, Billy's daddy, had stayed true to his promise by having Ed disappear into the night just hours after Sheriff had returned me home from the jailhouse. That was the last time I saw my brother in the flesh.

Of course, the press had made a big deal about his disappearance, but with all three perpetrators now missing—the Benson boys had mysteriously disappeared on their own accord, although, from what I had heard, not under the direction and guidance of Attorney General Jennings, but perhaps Sheriff—the state was forced to drop any plans for a retrial.

I had spent the last five years trying hard to love Billy Jennings. Billy Jr. was the only thing keeping me from going insane or attempting to disappear myself. Now in Jackson, Billy was an up-and-coming defense attorney, his daddy's clout and status landing him a job with one of the top firms in the state. When Billy wasn't busy obsessing over the details of some high-profile case he and his firm were involved with, he was busy constructing his eventual plans to run for Mississippi state governor. When he wasn't doing either, he was usually finding new and inventive ways to beat and rape me.

My role as Billy Jennings's relentlessly sexually abused wife began on our wedding night. Billy's daddy had paid for us a week's stay at a New Orleans hotel suite; a honeymoon of forced interactions and living nightmares. I had barely made it into the room that first night, when Billy kicked my feet from below me, forcing me to the ground. He pressed his fist against my mouth before I could cry out, the forcing of his manhood inside me rough and damaging. I had spent the rest of our wedding night tiptoeing to the bathroom to clean the droplets of blood that continuously trickled out of me, the physical reminder of the trauma I had just endured. I took a very long look at myself in the mirror that night, observing the face of a woman who had just suffered the second sexual assault of her life; a tally that was soon to become far too enormous to keep track of. Countless nights, Billy would return home from a stressful day at the office, punch me directly in the face, force me against some piece of furniture, and have his way with me. I had lost track of the nights I would awake to find him on top of me, ragefully fulfilling his insatiable sexual desires with the unwilling and previously unconscious participation of my body. Billy Jr. was my miracle lifesaver, arriving just in time to keep me from being completely unable to continue handling my hellish existence. I knew with certainty that my son was the only reason I was still alive.

"Hey, Momma, watch me!" I heard my son say, freeing me from the relentless chatter of my brain. I looked up to see him covered in a mixture of playground sand, dirt, chocolate fudge, and cotton candy. Our backyard had been completely overhauled into a fairground circus. Balloon-twisting clowns and various animals and portable amusement rides, as well as an entire set of performers and staff, were hired to operate the function properly. I sat beside my sister, who had moved with us to Jackson from Waynesboro, which occurred just less than a year from Billy's and my first wedding anniversary. Francis dominated the entire east wing of our far too large and overstated Mississippi manor. The house was enormous, a grand and overzealous reminder of Mississippi's plantation past. I imagined that the ghosts of Southern belles and hardworking slaves haunted the corners of the open fields that surrounded the mansion, as well as the lonely corridors which acted as the structure's veins.

"I'm gonna go freshen up," Francis said, rising from her lawn chair and sashaying toward the house. Without a job or stable beau to speak of, Francis spent most of her time enjoying the spoils and splendor of Billy's family and personal wealth. Billy and I had been married just under a year when I first discovered evidence of Billy and Francis's affair. Billy kept their meetings secret, but Francis was careless and bold in her discretion, or lack thereof. I never confronted either of them. In fact, I relished the time and attention Billy spent on Francis. I had my son to tend to, my soul's life purpose. Plus, I didn't marry Billy for love anyhow. I know it sounds crazy or plain insane, but despite the ongoing sexual and physical abuse, I had a comfortable life. I didn't have to work, and I was able to devote nearly all of my time to my son and his well-being.

"Can I get ya anything, Mrs. Jennings?" I heard a meek voice ask. I looked up to see Mae Chambers, our live-in housemaid. She was a young colored girl, perhaps twenty. I had never asked her exact age, and she never revealed it. She had been hired to clean and care for Billy Jr., but I relieved her of most of the latter responsibility. Mae and I were friends, if you could define it as such. Despite her stance as a household employee, I relied on and confided in her. Her company was often the only adult companionship I had. It was impossible for me to ever count the number of times Mae would find me on the master bathroom floor after passing out there after one of Billy's tirades. Oftentimes, his rage and fury were so intense, so great, he would knock me unconscious, usually with his fists, but sometimes at the cause of his vigorous sexual thrusting. I knew it better not to resist him; I had stopped trying just weeks into the marriage. In reality, I did not know what it was like for a man to make love to me. In the few instances where Billy was actually thoughtful and gentle with me, his selfish focus and need for specific pleasures still isolated and alienated my personal physical or emotional needs. As a woman of twenty-six, I had yet to ever experience an orgasm by a man.

"No, thank ya, Mae. I was just gonna head inside myself."

Mae smiled, her eyes warm and friendly. I knew she had no other choice but to be kind to me. I was her employer after all. But I felt in my heart that Mae truly cared for me, as I did her, and that there was something unique and genuine in our connection.

"Okay, ma'am," she replied before tending to the mess of food-stained plates and utensils on a nearby picnic table.

I made light and friendly conversations with many of the mothers of Billy Jr.'s playmates as I journeyed back toward the house. I wasn't close nor personal with any of them. Most were married to the other attorneys in Billy's firm or were wives of the Jackson aristocrats that made up the neighborhood. Despite their genteel manners and conversation, I found most of them to be superficial and boring, if not disingenuous and false in their convictions. Still, I played the part. The last thing I ever wanted to do was to give Billy yet another reason to beat me.

The muffled sounds of the birthday party slowly faded as I ascended the grand staircase to the second floor. I kicked off my heels as I entered the master suite, the sound of moaning gripping my attention. I looked up to see Billy, Francis on her knees before him, a look of passion sealing his eyes and gaping his mouth. I turned to exit the room, when I heard Billy say my name.

"Judy," he barked, the sound of his voice sending chills down my spine. Hesitantly, I turned to face him.

Francis was still on her knees, a smirking expression accenting her lipstick-smudged mouth. Billy was busy re-fastening his pants.

"What're ya doin' up here?" he continued. "Whaddya want?"

"I came to change my shoes, Billy," I answered dryly, moving my head in the opposite direction. It no longer pained me to encounter these types of situations. It didn't even disgust me anymore. If anything, I had become numb and immune to the humiliation.

"Well, next time . . . ya best knock."

Without thought or hesitation, I heard my reply fall from my lips, unfiltered and unedited.

"It's my own room, Billy, I ain't gonna knock."

I could feel the sting of his open hand a full thirty seconds before he moved to strike me. I opened my eyes to see Francis standing behind Billy, her face twisted in a familiar scowl.

"Don't start with ya shit, girl," he seethed, his brilliant-white teeth glowing. "I ain't in the mood for ya mouth today."

I knelt to fetch my heels and turned to leave the room.

"Don'tcha walk away from me!" I heard Billy shout, just moments before he kicked my feet from below me. I felt my left front tooth puncture my upper lip as my chin slammed against the wooden floor of the hallway.

I opened my eyes to see my sister's feet moving over my head and into the distance beyond. My last visual memory was that of her smirking face as she turned her head over her shoulder for one last glance.

The sound of the master suite door slamming shut was the last thing I heard after Billy dragged me into the room. I kept my eyes closed as the expected blows met my hips and ribcage. With guests just feet away downstairs, I knew Billy would avoid striking my face with his fists, for fear of leaving marks and bruises. Whenever I was needed to be seen in public, he reserved his fury to the places of my body that would be concealed by the expensive clothing he routinely bought for me.

After Billy was through, I crawled to the master bathroom and struggled to lift myself up the side of the sink counter. I had just begun splashing cold water over the crimson slap mark across my pale cheek, when I felt someone place a hand on my right shoulder. I opened my eyes to see Mae.

"Lemme help ya, Mrs. Jennings," she whispered, moving to fetch a fresh washcloth.

"I'm fine, really," I responded, still hunched over the sink. I attempted to stand straight, but the fresh bruises of Billy's kick marks fired their presence over my stomach and ribcage. Succumbing to the pain, I remained still.

"Do ya think I'm a fool?" I heard myself ask Mae as she carefully dabbed the cool washcloth over my face.

"No ma'am, I would neva' think that of ya, Mrs. Jennings."

I opened my eyes to see the young girl smiling at me nervously.

"Five years now, Mae," I continued, reclosing my eyes as the washcloth again touched the surface of Billy's handprint. "Five years I've lived like this."

Mae didn't respond. She continued to cycle the damp cloth over the same three sections of my face, focusing mostly on the quickly swelling slap mark.

"He told me he'd kill me," I continued, uttering the same words I had already confessed to Mae on previous similar occasions. "He said he'd always find me and kill me. He said I could neva' take his son away from him."

"Shh, Mrs. Jennings. I know," Mae cooed, inching her face a bit closer to mine.

"He could do it too, Mae. He could kill me and get away with it."

I had long suspected Billy's involvement in Ezra's murder. I no longer doubted that it was indeed Billy who had attacked me in the woods that night. I had begun piecing it all together just weeks into the routine beatings and rapes. The way Billy would kick my feet out from below me. The way he opted to assault me from behind. It was all the same as the memory of what had occurred that rainy night in the woods. I believe Ezra had been following me, carefully observing from a distance, concerned for my well-being due to my emotional reaction to his revelation just prior to that night, the revelation that society would never allow us to be together, at least not in peace, and that I was better off accepting the courtship of a boy like Billy Jennings. I believe Ezra had tried to stop Billy that night. That was why I had heard his voice. I believe Billy then sent Ed, who involved the Benson brothers, after Ezra. None of this had made any sense to me prior to the marriage. After the occurrence in the woods, while still in the hospital, the idea of Billy attacking me had only once entered my brain, but quickly dissipated. Five years of the same assault had confirmed it though. Of course, I never said a word of any of this to Billy. In all the five years we had been married, the name Ezra, Ed, nor mention of the trial had ever once come up. Still, I knew in my soul that Billy had been involved somehow. Whatever the details, I was still uncertain, but I just knew his hands were just as stained with Ezra's blood as Ed's and the Benson brothers'.

"I stay to protect my son, Mae." I sobbed softly. "I stay for him."

As with so many nights before, Mae simply tended to my wounds and soothed my crying. Never once did she judge me. Yet, never once did she ever agree with my decision to stay.

An hour later, I was standing next to Billy and Francis as an enormous baseball-themed birthday cake was wheeled out from the kitchen. The crowd of guests, which included Billy's parents, all applauded as my son gleefully blew out his candles. Billy gripped my shoulder and planted a gentle kiss on my forehead as the approving audience looked on.

I poked at my slice of cake as various conversations went on around me. The smell of caked-on face powder assaulted my nose to the point where I could no longer taste the bits of sugar-heavy pastry morsels I cautiously slipped over my tongue. Mae had attempted to cover the slap mark the best she could, adding enough powder and rouge to suffice the various clowns that still twisted their balloons in different sections of the massive dining room.

The crowd began to disperse thirty minutes or so after Billy Jr. energetically tore open his mountain of birthday gifts. I looked on with a frozen smile, nodding and obliging those who tossed thoughtless, polite comments my way.

"He's such a handsome young thing!" one of the overdressed neighbor wives commented. "He most certainly has his daddy's good looks!"

I cringed inside yet stayed faithful to my smile. I hated the comparisons to Billy when it came to Billy Jr. I wanted nothing more for my son than to turn out to be everything his father wasn't. I was careful to never vilify Billy to his namesake son. The boy was still far too young to understand. Yet, it was hard to tout praise for the man who routinely beat and assaulted the young boy's mother. Thankfully, Billy Jr. had yet to witness his father ever striking me. At least Billy had enough thought and dignity to spare his son the trauma.

Mae and I tended to the dishes while the rest of the birthday staff packed their games, rides, and concession stands and headed out. It was when I was alone in the pantry that my sister approached me.

"It was a lovely party, Sista." She grinned, placing her body before the pantry doorway so I could not escape.

"Yes, thank ya, Francis," I murmured, avoiding her eyes as best I could.

"I hope ya aren't too upset about earlia'," she continued, nervously spinning her oversized pearls, which dangled pridefully around her neck. "Billy and I try and keep things discrete, ya know."

"I'm fine, Francis. Thank ya. Now, would ya please—"

"There's a letta'," Francis interrupted, pinning her arms between herself and the pantry doorframe. I had no choice but to continue listening to her. "A letta' arrived from Waynesboro."

We connected eyes, her usual dazzle of defiance and pride suddenly diming to what appeared to be kindness and sympathy.

"It's from that colored boy's momma," she continued, her smirk returning slightly. "I found it in Billy's office. I don't suppose he was gonna give it to ya. I have it though."

Francis and I observed each other's expression without movement or sound.

"I will say, I didn't realize Negro folk could write that well. I swear, this woman is more literate than me."

She laughed to herself for a few seconds before silencing to my expressionless stare.

"Well, hell, Sista," she continued, shifting her weight in the doorframe, "I'm tryin' to do somethin' nice for ya here. I figured seein' this letta' would mean somethin' to ya. I know ya still have a soft spot for that dead boy. Despite everything."

"Where's the letta'?" I asked dryly, preparing myself to have to interrogate her.

"I have it," Francis fired back, her gleaming eyes confirming her power and position over me. Even though I was the wife of the household, Francis dominated me as if I were no more than a low-wage servant.

"Are ya gonna give it to me, Francis?" I asked, my stomach suddenly turning with nervousness. I had never forgotten Ms. Washington's intense and palpable stares during the trial. They still haunted my dreams today just as much as they did then.

"Depends," Francis teased, her usual grinning smirk returning to her face. "I want the gold broach Billy gave you last Motha's Day. The one with the diamond edges."

"Fine," I agreed without hesitating. "It's yours."

"Yay!" Francis cheered, clapping her hands quietly like a spoiled child rewarded with yet another undeserved treat. "Meet me back here around midnight. I'll give it to ya then."

Francis departed the pantry doorway, freeing me to resume my mind-distracting chores with Mae. I was never asked to assist Mae with her daily or special event duties. I did so out of equal respect for someone I considered a friend, and out of the desperation to escape my present reality. It was ten thirty or so by the time I finally retired to the master suite. Billy was already in bed when I got there, his face buried in a pile of work papers. My heart lifted in relief at his distraction.

"You should bathe," he suggested without looking up. His words froze me in place.

"Ya have far too much rouge on," he continued, finally lifting his eyes to meet mine. "Ya look like one of the clowns that was here earlia'. Go wash it off."

I resisted responding. I silently moved into the bathroom and began splashing warm water over my still-sore cheeks. I was nearly through when Billy appeared behind me.

"Do ya still love me?" he asked, his voice stern yet somehow gentle and concerned. "Did ya eva' love me?"

My heart began to race. I had not prepared for any conversation with Billy, much less one of this magnitude and sensitivity.

I blinked rapidly as my brain scurried to find the appropriate words. Not the words of truth, but the words that would avoid a beating, or at least earn me a less severe one.

"Yes, um . . . Billy. Yes, I still love ya."

My words fell from my throat as vacant and hollow as an old, dead tree. I knew immediately that Billy didn't believe me.

Expecting an outburst, I was shocked when he instead fell to his knees in a sob.

"I know that ain't true," he mumbled through visible tears. "I know ya neva' loved me."

I didn't know what to do. I could only look at him, the complete disbelief over what I was seeing trying its best to register within my brain. In the entire time I had known Billy, I had never once seen him shed a tear about anything, much less about me. Even when Billy Jr. was born, Billy was far more concerned with getting back to his weekly poker game and lighting up celebratory stogies with his fellow players.

I flinched as Billy suddenly crawled forward and wrapped his arms around my ankles. Like a child desperate for his mother's approval, he continued to sob and heave uncontrollably. Forcing myself to overcome my understandable surprise, I lowered my knees until he was able to wrap his arms around my shoulders.

"I've loved ya since the first time I eva' laid eyes on ya," he whispered through his sobs. "You were the only girl in high school who didn't seem to care about me. That made me want ya. Everything about ya. All I've eva' wanted was for ya to love me the same."

My heart felt like it was going to leap up my throat and out my mouth as I frantically tried to comprehend what was happening around me. Never in ten lifetimes did I ever imagine witnessing Billy Jennings sobbing at my feet.

"Please forgive me for eva' hurtin' ya," he begged, his red, swollen, tearstained face now an inch or so from mine. "Please, tell me ya forgive me."

I shook my head, trying desperately to form words. Any words. But I only made way for the passage of uncontrolled and uncensored truth.

"How can I love a man who stole everything from me?" I heard myself ask, the echo of my voice bouncing off the pristine glossy tiles of the master bathroom.

A slight tinge of rage circled Billy's eyes. Expecting a blow, I unconsciously pulled myself back in his arms.

"No," he spoke, lowering his eyes in apparent shame, "ya right."

Without thought, my voice seized the unfathomable opportunity. I felt I was outside my body, watching and listening to myself unload on him.

"Ya've stolen so much from me, Billy. My innocence. The first man I eva' loved."

The words swirled and echoed around the oversized bathroom like an angry tornado roaring over a single house.

"Despite what ya said in ya witness statement at the time, I know ya told Ed it was Ezra who had raped me. My sista told me ya did. But it was you, Billy. You attacked me in the woods that night, and you caused Ed and the Benson boys to murda' Ezra."

Billy pulled himself back, his face slowly morphing into his usual sturdy expression.

"Is that where ya take this?" he questioned, slightly cocking his head to one side. "I fall on my knees before ya, beggin' for ya forgiveness for not treatin' ya right, and ya bring this back to that dead nigga boy?"

I felt myself re-enter my body, scrambling to somehow gain control of my mouth.

"It's him, isn't it?" Billy continued, nodding his head at his own conclusion. "Ya neva' stopped lovin' him."

A stream of steady, certain tears began to soak my face. I didn't sob. I didn't even lose my breath.

"How could I eva' stop lovin' him when I was neva' even given a chance to say goodbye?"

Too much. I had said way too much. I knew it even before Billy gripped his hand around my throat. I knew it well before he began slamming the back of my head against the solid wood cabinet it rested on.

"I give ya everything!" Billy shouted, his face again just a mere inch or so from mine. "Ya live in the most beautiful house in Jackson . . . a closet full of the nicest clothes. Jewelry, furniture . . . ya neva' need for nothin'. Yet all I get in return is you accusin' me of rapin' ya and causin' a murda'! I marry-up the town nigga-lovin' whore and this is the thanks I get!"

I started to blackout, when Billy finally released my throat. To my surprise, he didn't strike further. Instead, he pressed his face tightly against mine, our noses and skin mashed like dough under a rolling pin.

"Why won't ya love me like ya loved him?" he cried, fresh tears oozing between our smashed cheeks. "What can I do to make ya love me like ya loved him?"

I could hardly breathe, Billy's nose and lips pressed so tightly against my own.

"Huh!" he screamed, the taste of his mouth glazing over my lips. "Tell me! I wanna know what it is! What can I do! What is it about him that I don't have!"

I didn't dare respond. My mouth had gotten me into far too much trouble as it was. Still, the echo of my own voice filling the bathroom again resounded within my ears.

"Because he was true to me," I heard myself say, calm and certain.

Billy pulled back, inspecting my face curiously.

"What does that mean?" he whispered in a semi-growl.

I was too afraid to respond, but knew full well that I currently had no control over the things my brain popped off my tongue like overheated popcorn kernels. Five years of silence had finally burst like the head of a long-festering boil.

"He cared about me. He listened to me. He did the things with me that I loved," I stated.

Billy continued to inspect my expression, his eyes darting over every inch of my face as if viewing it for the very first time. To my complete disbelief, he still did not strike me.

"Like baseball?" he asked quietly, his voice so innocent and clueless that it sounded like Billy Jr.'s.

"Yes." I nodded. "Like baseball."

I saw the familiar spiral of rage make its worn and repeated trek around his pupils. Still, he resisted it, instead rising to his feet, even reaching out his hand toward me.

"Come," he said softly. "Let's go to bed."

Billy was gentle that night in the way he pleasured himself with my body. I would hesitate to consider it lovemaking, as I was never quite certain what that even was, but it wasn't the same as the usual assaults or even the less severe occasions of more subtle thrusting. No. This was different. In fact, I could feel him sobbing as he orgasmed, the surge of his seed bursting a fresh well of salt-heavy water from his eyes.

I felt Billy fade off to sleep, the echoes of his voice and mine replaying the scene that had only just occurred in the bathroom less than an hour before. It wasn't until my head drifted to the side and I was able to view the glowing clock on the nightstand, that I snapped out of my thoughts. Twelve thirty. I had forgotten all about Francis.

Scurrying to locate my nightgown, I tiptoed to the massive jewelry case, sifting my fingers over the treasure of silver, gold, and diamonds in search of the broach I had promised my sister. Finally locating it, I slipped it into my nightgown pocket and tiptoed downstairs. To my surprise, Francis was still in the kitchen waiting for me.

"I been waitin'," she sighed as I neared her. She took one glance at my disheveled hair and face before concluding, "Anotha' Billy moment?"

I didn't reply, but instead allowed her to settle with her own assumption. I flipped the broach onto the counter and reached out my hand.

"Where's the letta'?" I asked, watching my sister as she scooped up the expensive piece of jewelry like a peanut-hungry squirrel.

"It's just there," she nodded. I followed her lead to the nearby cookie jar. "It's in the jar."

Before I could utter a word, Francis flowed out of the kitchen, her draping black silk robe gliding on the air behind her.

I wasted no time in locating the letter.

It took me three times of reading it before I could fully absorb and understand the message Ms. Washington was trying to convey. It wasn't due to her penmanship or writing quality, for, as Francis had mentioned, she came across as highly intelligent and articulate. Despite whatever limited education she most likely had, her words flowed with purity, ease, and elegance.

The letter began with Ms. Washington admitting that she had spent several years blaming me solely for her son's death. She said she couldn't help but assume I had somehow led her son on with false hope and promises, all the while knowing full well we could never actually be together. She said it was a dream that had changed her mind. A dream where Ezra came to her, urging her to forgive me. She said it inspired her to write the letter, despite the massive personal risk it took. She just felt she had to somehow let me know that she no longer harbored blame nor hatred in her heart toward me. Only love and forgiveness.

After my third time through the letter, I collapsed on the floor, my tears as strong and heavy as the first time I heard that a body had been found in the mud of a Wayne County creek. A headless, brutalized body that I just knew for certain was my Ezra.

I read the letter another dozen or so times before collecting myself and returning to the master suite. Much to my relief, Billy was sound asleep, snoring as loudly as a motorboat chugging along on a circular pond.

I slipped the letter into the bottom of the massive jewelry chest, placing over it as many necklaces, rings, jewels, and trinkets as I could, and returned to the bed.

I didn't dream that night, although the spiraling vision of Ms. Washington's words of love and forgiveness zigzagged behind my lids as I slowly and cautiously gave in to sleep.

There was something distinctly different about Billy that next day. He brought me breakfast in bed, referred to me as "sweetheart" and "sweetie" at every single opportunity, and even seemed to bypass or ignore Francis whenever they were both in my presence.

It was nearly dusk when he forced me to cover my eyes and escorted me to the furthest corner of the seemingly endless backyard.

Uncovering my eyes, I saw the beginnings of a baseball field. Mounds of bright orange clay next to various piles of chain-link fence and metal poles littered the scene before me. I shook my head in disbelief before turning to face a brightly beaming Billy.

"Whaddya think?" he asked, his face so bright with joy that I hardly even recognized him.

"Uh . . . wow, Billy . . . I . . . uh . . ."

My fluttering response only seemed to annoy him. Instantly, the beaming expression fell into one of impatience and annoyance.

"It's a baseball field, Judy," he stated plainly. "I had 'em start work on it this mornin'. Obviously, it ain't finished yet, but it's gonna be state of the art once completed. Far betta' than that makeshift dirt hole you use to play on back in the colored side of Waynesboro."

I just looked at him, screaming at myself on the inside to force a smile.

"Wow, Billy," I said breathlessly, shaking my head and fluttering my eyelids. "I truly don't know what to say."

"Say ya grateful," he snapped. "Say ya appreciate the kindness and thought that went into this."

I couldn't speak. A sudden lock of terror gripped my throat tighter than Billy had the night before.

Desperate, I forced a nod and a smile, my words completely failing me.

"I was thinkin' you and some of the otha' wives could play ball out here once in a while. Ya know, have ya own little ladies league or whateva'."

I toured my eyes over the half-finished field, laughing to myself at the very thought of the frigid, uppity, over-fragile wives of his fellow lawyers or those of the neighborhood ever attempting to play baseball. Still, I continued to smile and nod, too afraid to do anything to upset him given the odd and unexpected circumstances. Something was different about him since last night, and though I most certainly did not ease into complacency or any sort of security about it, I still did not want to conjure any form of outburst or upset.

"That sounds wonderful, Billy. I'd love that."

I smiled and nodded, trying my best to react the way he wanted me to.

I listened as Billy rattled off various details regarding the proposed dugout, scoreboard, bleachers, and even a concession. He had really put a lot of thought into this and had pulled together quite a feat in organizing and delegating the project.

He draped an arm over my shoulder as we walked back toward the house. I saw Francis in one of the upstairs windows, peering down at us with a foreign and unfamiliar glare.

It wasn't until she got me alone that she said something about it.

"So, what was all that about?" she asked coldly, cornering me in Billy Jr.'s bathroom, where I was giving the young boy a bath.

"Uh, what?" I asked, for whatever reason finding it best to play stupid with her.

"Ya know what I'm talkin' about," she snapped, her eyes glazed with the evidence of drinking. "Why did Billy take ya out into the field? Y'all seemed pretty lovely-dovey as ya came back up to the house."

"He's building me a baseball field," I replied matter-of-factly, knowing the admission was bound to bring about another slew of questions.

"Oh, really," Francis smirked. "Just like the good ol' days with ya nigga boyfriend."

I didn't respond nor turn around. Instead, I focused a smile at Billy Jr. as he nonchalantly continued to live out his escape in his own private world of imagination.

"Whaddya think'a that letta'?" Francis continued once she saw her original statement received no response. "Ya gonna write her back?"

I could hear clanking behind me, realizing Francis had brought the crystal whiskey set from Billy's office. It wasn't until I heard her down another mouthful of the brown liquid, that she pestered me further.

"I think ya should," she stated, her voice suddenly alive and vibrant. "Ya should just be honest with her. Write her back, Sista. I support it."

I turned on my knees to face her, the glittering dazzle of whiskey tears glimmering in her eyes.

"Oh, ya support it? And why is that, Francis?"

Francis shifted her eyes around the room, obviously altering and censoring her reply.

"Because I love ya, Sista," she finally spoke. "Despite what you may think, I do love ya, and I want the best for ya. I wanna see ya be able to heal and finally move past all this. I know ya still hold a sore spot in ya heart over that whole ordeal with that colored boy."

I didn't respond. I was too disinterested and tired to attempt decoding her true and more than likely selfish intentions.

"Most of all, dear Sista," she whispered, the whiskey on her breath so heavy that I could smell it nearly two feet away, "I know ya still feel guilty about it. Perhaps admittin' that to this boy's momma will help ya. Ya should tell her everything. I think the poor woman deserves to know the whole truth."

She waited for a moment before stumbling toward me.

"Only you can give her the whole truth, Sista. Only you can express to her the way ya really felt about her son. I think that will help provide her some closure. Ya know, knowing her son was loved in an honest way and all."

The sound of Billy Jr.'s playing faded into the space behind my ears. Perhaps it was only the liquor talking, but I was somehow connecting to this sudden and unexpected moment of potentially authentic honesty from my sister.

"I think ya right," I whispered, my reply causing her to smile.

"Of course I'm right!" she declared, rising to her feet as she spoke. "Ya wouldn't be livin' the life'a luxury ya have if it wasn't for me. I mean, come on, do ya really think Billy boy would still be puttin' up with ya frigid ass if it wasn't for me around takin' the brunt of all his overbearin' needs?"

She laughed to herself before playfully kicking at my side.

"Hey, you may be the one he loves, but I'm the one who keeps him satisfied."

Instead of responding, I turned my attention back to my son and continued to bathe him.

"Well, anyhow, Sista," Francis proceeded, shuffling her way toward the bathroom door, "I really think ya should write her back. Tell her everything. Don't hold back. As I said, she deserves to know the truth."

I heard her open the door and begin to exit.

"Only you can give her that."

She didn't wait for a reply. She closed Billy Jr.'s bathroom door and could be heard shuffling down the hallway.

Francis's suggestion lingered with me as I finished with Billy Jr.'s bath and dressed him for bed. I hadn't really thought about responding to Ms. Washington. Perhaps because I had only just been able to fully absorb and understand her need to reveal her truth to me.

Francis was right though. The still-grieving mother did deserve to know the truth. My truth. And as my sister so surprisingly said, only I could give it to her.

The house was quiet the next morning when I sat down to write my letter to Ms. Washington. Billy was at a court hearing, Francis a hair appointment, and Billy Jr. on his way to kindergarten with Mae. I found it far easier to just allow Mae to drop Billy Jr. off each morning. Seeing that it was his first year of school, I did have quite a hard time adjusting to his absence from the house each week day. Billy Jr. seemed to ease into his routine a bit easier when it was Mae dropping him off at school instead of his mother. With me, he tended to cling to my side and hesitate. The first week was by far the hardest. Seeing my one and only son beg and cry for me not to leave him was more than heartbreaking. I spent that entire first week sauntering around the house, crying spontaneously, desperately missing my son as though he had been kidnapped from me. Thank

God for Mae, for she certainly made that first adjustment phase far easier for both mother and son by acting as a buffer in overtaking the morning drop-off ritual. I got to serve and enjoy Billy Jr. as he chattily consumed his breakfast each morning. I even made sure I was the one to pack his lunch and dress him. Mae tended to Billy Sr.'s morning breakfast routine, allowing me full freedom to the motherly duties many women in my position of privilege willingly and gratefully left to their hired help.

It took a while, but I was finally able to prick some place deep with myself and allow my soul to write the letter. Each word, each sentence, each paragraph, everything flowed with pure honesty and truth. I held nothing back. I told Ms. Washington everything: the secret hours spent in the old cemetery deep in the woods, my admission of love to Ezra, even his acceptance of the unfortunate truth of our circumstances. I detailed for her the last time I saw Ezra, how he selflessly assured my well-being despite going against what I was certain his heart was telling him. I even found myself confessing my continued love for him, how I still thought of him, dreamt of him, longed for him. I confessed my guilt at not being able to do more during the trial, and even my personal shame regarding my brother, Ed's, involvement; despite how much I desperately missed him. I left out the deal I had made with Mr. Jennings, the state attorney general. Something in me didn't feel the need to confess that bit, so I instead focused on the honesty and truth of my love and grieving for her Ezra. Several tears smudged my signature as I gracefully signed my name to the bottom of the last page. Three full pages, front and back, of channeled writing now sat on the desk before me. As I read the letter back, I was amazed at the power and depth of my words. It was almost as if someone else had written it. Each word bled with the sorrow of my heart. I just knew the voice of my soul had moved and controlled my hand as the black ink spread across the page. A part of me felt somehow relieved as I saw my five-year pent-up truth dutifully scrawled over the stationary. I allowed myself several minutes of sobbing before collecting my composure in anticipation of someone's returning. I didn't have the courage to try to explain or lie about my tearful appearance to either my sister or Mae. I collected the letter carefully, hiding it beneath the pile of jewelry that hid and contained Ms. Washington's original letter. Splashing my face with cold water, I adjusted my hair and blouse and dashed downstairs. I enjoyed the sudden and unexpected sense of freedom I felt for the rest of the afternoon. Writing the letter to Ms. Washington had been deeply and profoundly cathartic. Five years of silent suffering seemed to bleed out of me like infected blood from some long-festering wound. I decided to celebrate the feeling further by treating myself to a late-afternoon shopping spree. Mae had completed her afternoon duties and was on her way to pick up Billy Jr. from school, and Francis had yet to return from her morning hair appointment. Billy Sr. wasn't expected home till after dusk, so I made the most of my time by slipping into one of Billy's various sports cars, my personal favorite his brand-new 1962 Chevrolet Corvette C2, and drove to Jackson.

Every single head turned and every face gawked as I parked the magnificent car in front of Swanson's Pastry Cafe and walked inside. Most everyone in Jackson knew who I was, the wife of one of the city's most successful and influential defense attorneys, not to mention the scarred and infamous victim of a still hotly debated and lightning-rod topic of one of Mississippi's most notorious unsolved and unfinished criminal cases. I normally avoided going into town for this very reason, especially alone, but something inside me felt different today; something felt free and uninhibited.

I was sitting alone near the front window of the cafe, slowly enjoying a freshly baked croissant and newly brewed cup of black dark-roast coffee, when a familiar voice sent chills down every single millimeter of my spine.

"That's quite the car you have there, Mrs. Jennings."

I looked up to see Luke Pinder, his familiar, handsome face smiling down at me. My heart skipped and flittered a bit before leaping into a nervous pounding.

"May I sit down?" he asked after I failed to respond, my mouth too full of pastry and my brain too filled with shock to conjure any sensible words. Forcing myself into the moment, I smiled and nodded, quickly swallowing the last bits of softened croissant that still lay upon my tongue.

"Luke," I managed to sputter as he took the small white iron chair beside me. "What're . . . ?"

"Surprised to see me?" he chimed in after my words trailed into the unknown.

I had not seen Luke since that last day of the trial, the one where Ed had admitted his guilt to the unsuspecting courthouse. Luke had been summoned back to Meridian that night, the district attorney himself planning to overtake the case as it headed toward the expected retrial. With Ed and the Benson boys disappearing, I hadn't heard tale of either the DA nor his assistant, Mr. Luke Pinder, since early 1958, when the case finally cooled and the press lost interest.

"What're ya doin' here?" I managed to mumble, quickly gripping the handle of my coffee mug for a gulp of black liquid. I winced as the heat of the smoldering molten mass made its way over my tongue and down my throat.

"Easy there, Judy," Luke laughed, retrieving the napkin the mug had been resting on and using it to dab the corner of my mouth. My heart began to beat faster as the long-missing, familiar fragrance of Luke's aftershave gently glided below the skin of my nose.

"How're you doing, my friend?" he whispered.

I fluttered my lashes and lowered my face as it began to heat to the crimson tide of embarrassment. It took me several seconds before I was again able to muster the use of my voice.

"I'm well, Luke. How are ya?"

He smiled his infectious smile and replaced the napkin back onto the table. Gently, he took the coffee mug from my slightly shaking hand and replaced it atop the napkin.

"It's okay, Judy," he whispered, leaning his face closer to mine. "Don't be nervous to see me."

My eyes flicked over his head and into the distance of the pastry shop behind him. As suspected, every patron was looking our way, chit-chatting to whomever was nearby.

"I don't think it's a good idea that we talk here," I whispered, without returning my eyes to Luke's. "Too many talkin' eyes around."

Understanding my concern, Luke pulled a pen from his front shirt pocket and proceeded to scribble a phone number onto the edge of the coffee mug napkin.

"Please," he whispered, sliding the napkin and mug closer to me. "Call me. I'd really like to speak with you."

He didn't wait for a response as he lifted from the chair and disappeared from the cafe. The staring eyes of the onlookers remained heavy on me as I folded the napkin into my purse and returned to the Corvette. Several Jackson residents flocked around the vehicle, obnoxiously gawking at its brilliance.

"Excuse me," I squeaked as I slid through the tiny crowd and to the car door.

"I suppose that's the compensation ya get for bein' a nigga lova'," I heard one of the men grumble to his comrades just as I slammed the car door shut. Inhaling deeply, I closed my eyes, fired the ignition, and floored the accelerator, tossing the gearshift into reverse. Refusing to even glance back at the ogling gaggle of onlookers, I bumped the engine into drive and peeled away.

Thankfully, Billy was still not home as I carefully glided the car back inside his five-car garage. Francis was waiting for me near the back door as I tried unsuccessfully to slip into the house unnoticed.

"Heard ya was in town today," she blurted the moment I was near enough to hear her.

"Huh?" I automatically replied, nervous but mostly annoyed at her presence.

"Word on the street is that ya took ya'self a little stroll into town all by ya lonesome with one of Billy's new cars. Are ya sure he's gonna be okay with that?"

"Francis," I sighed, untying the headscarf from around my head and nervously adjusting my pearl earrings. "I'm in no mood for ya questions just now."

She scoffed and stepped aside as I shoved past her to enter the kitchen.

"Whatever," she said in a singsong voice. "I suppose it was ya right to just take the car without ya husband's permission. It's also ya' face his fist is gonna land on once he finds out."

I ignored her as I kicked off my flats and knelt to retrieve them. I was nearly to my closet, when the slightly open door of the massive jewelry case caught my eye. Terrified, I tiptoed toward it, slowly opening the door and fishing through the drawer that contained both letters.

"Lookin' for ya letta's?" I heard Francis ask from the doorway.

"Francis, seriously now. What have ya done with 'em?"

"My, my, Mrs. Jennings," she continued to speak in a singsong voice, her eyes glowing like smoldering charcoal as I slowly walked toward her. "I wonder what ya husband would think if he read just how much ya still in love with that dead nigga boy?"

Her words stopped me in my tracks.

"It'd be a shame if he was to somehow come into possession of a letta' of such admission."

"Francis, I'm warnin' ya. I—"

"Warnin' me!" she shrieked, her voice reminiscent of a rodent as it is scooped from the roadside by some swooping bird of prey. "I believe I'm the one warnin' you, Mrs. Jennings."

My heart thudded so loudly inside my head that I could barely hear Francis's voice until she was standing just inches in front of me.

"Let's just say ya betta' stay on my good side, dear Sista," she hissed with a smirking whisper. "I'd truly hate to see what would happen to ya if Mr. Jennings was to somehow find ya letter."

She spun on her high heels and flopped her steps over the thick carpet toward the door.

"Rememba' who has the powa' to eitha' make or not make that happen."

I started to speak just as Francis clicked the door shut behind her. Panicked, I sifted through the whirlwind inside my mind, desperate for the answer on what to do next. I knew there was no way Francis would return the letters simply by me demanding them from her, nor would a tearful barrage of begging do much to persuade her. My heart sank into my core as I surrendered to the fact that my sister now held me in the palm of her hand by the constraints of her selfish control and sadistic mind games. I knew there was nothing I could do now but wait, hoping and praying she would eventually decide upon some expensive gift Billy had bought for me and would again exchange what she held from me for it. Something inside me warned that it was not going to be so easy this time around.

Abandoning the jewelry case as a trusted hiding spot, I tucked the cafe napkin with Luke Pinder's phone number written on it into the toe of one of my countless pairs of shoes and buried it deep within the furthest corner of my insanely large closet.

Dashing into the master bathroom, I slipped into the tub and began to mentally prepare myself to face Billy and Francis at the dinner table.

Quickly sliding into one of my many simple, sensible evening dresses, I piled my hair high on my head, refastened a string of pearls, patted my face with a bit of powder and rouge, and descended to the dining room. In the distance, I could hear Francis laughing behind the voice of Billy, her apparent interest and reaction to whatever it was he was saying an obvious audible warning to me that I was about to enter the risk zone.

Much to my surprise, and enormous relief, Francis never alluded to anything throughout not only the course of the dinner meal, but also even during the dessert and cleanup. Like always, I assisted Mae with the dishes as Billy retired to his study for a cigar and several glasses of brandy, and Billy Jr. enjoyed his last minutes of television before bedtime.

I didn't see Francis again for the rest of the evening, her words echoing loudly inside my head as I slipped myself beneath the covers and next to a soundly sleeping Billy. I knew it was only a matter of time before Francis cashed in her demands, and I could only pray as I fitfully drifted off to sleep that I would be able to appease and satiate them when that time came.

7

The Tree

It took me three full days to finally calm down enough to contemplate calling Luke Pinder. Once I realized Francis had no apparent intention to show Billy the letters, at least not yet anyway, I drifted into a sense of temporal peace that allowed me to venture outside my constant cage of worry and back into the daydream of possibility the sudden appearance of Luke had brought. It was late in the afternoon on the fourth day when I finally snuck to retrieve the napkin from my shoe and locked myself away in Billy's office to make the call.

Francis was off on one of her many all-day shopping sprees with her crusade of similarly shallow girlfriends, and Billy was out tending to details regarding his firm's latest case. Billy Jr. was already home from school. I had fed him a snack and set him before the television set before making my stealthy retrieval of the napkin.

With clunky and nervous fingers, I spun and re-spun the dial of Billy's dark green desktop telephone. It took me three attempts to dial the number properly, my heart beating too fast and my mind spinning too erratically for me to focus. After two rings, Luke Pinder's voice filled the receiver.

"I had a feeling it was you," he said softly after I said hello. "I knew it would take you a few days, but I knew for certain you would call me. I know you that well, Judy."

I smiled to myself, but made no mention of it as I forced myself into a stoic speaking voice.

"What do ya want from me, Luke?" I asked coldly, my nerves causing the phone to rattle against my pearl earring.

"I know, I'm sorry for just barging in on your life this way, Judy. I truly am. It's just . . . well, I promised myself I would be honest with you. I've spent the last five years doing a bit of side searching on my own time. I've never let this case go, Judy. I still think about what happened to Ezra every day, and I've made it my personal mission to track down and re-prosecute your brother and the Benson boys."

I sat in a stunned silence on the other end of the line, my shaking hand slowly giving way to annoyance and anger.

"I see, Mr. Pinder," I snapped, in my best impression of my sister. "I'd like to say I wish ya luck with that, but I don't."

I struggled to breathe as I formed my next sentence.

"I think it's best that ya just allow sleepin' corpses to lie . . . let him rest in peace."

"That's just the thing, Judy," Luke continued without skipping a beat. "How can Ezra ever truly be at rest when the men responsible for his murder are out living their lives as free people? How can his family ever secure some form of closure when justice has yet to be served?"

Again, I remained in my stunned silence, my heart pounding so loudly inside my head that I could feel it pressing against my temples.

"I want to know if you have any idea where your brother is, Judy," Luke continued, his voice wavering slightly in what sounded like nervousness. "I've resisted contacting you for five years, trying my best to find him on my own, but every lead turns out cold. I need your help, Judy. I know you still care about all this. Help me get justice for Ezra."

"Mr. Pinder," I stated in my most stern and clear voice, "I will only ask ya this one time and one time only. Please never contact me again. I want nothin' to do with ya or ya hunt for ghosts."

I started to replace the phone receiver over the cradle, when I heard Luke shout.

"Please, Judy! Please don't turn your back on me. I know you, Judy. You're a good girl. You have a good heart. I know all this still eats at you. It pecks at your soul day by day, year by year. Don't be eaten alive by this, Judy. Please help me do the right thing."

A rogue tear dripped down my face as I lowered the receiver completely, the clicking of the phone line's disconnection clear and audible even in the distance between my ear and the desktop telephone. Locating one of Billy's cigar lighters, I ignited the napkin and watched it burn to ashes in the center of Billy's massive crystal ashtray.

I was nearly to the door of the office, when Billy burst through.

"Hey, sweetie," he said softly, darting his eyes around the room. "What're ya in here for?"

My heart began to reaccelerate as I attempted to find my voice. I started blinking rapidly, visibly revealing my nerves as I stumbled to speak.

"I, uh . . . I was just . . . um . . ."

"It doesn't matta'," Billy replied, my shock and disbelief as printed and blatant over my expression as a newspaper headline.

"Come with me."

Billy grabbed my hand and pulled me along the corridor toward one of the various french doors which led into the backyard. He babbled carelessly as we journeyed the distance from the house to the back corner of the property.

"Whaddya think?" he cheerfully asked as we stepped onto the nearly completed baseball field.

Cautiously, I moved my head around to take in the full view of the scene before me. Two sets of bleachers aligned the sides of the field; a large, lamp-lit scoreboard towered over the edge of the now completed chain-link fence. Even a small concession booth accented the area next to the freshly painted dugout. The field was beautiful, its layout and design as vibrant and welcoming as any professional baseball field one sees in a sports magazine.

I nodded my head in approval, forcing a nervous smile out from behind my slightly chattering teeth and across my lipstick-less lips.

"It's beautiful, Billy. Wow," I forced myself to say.

Nodding his agreement, Billy pulled my hand and led me through each and every inch of the entire place. It wasn't until we neared the outfield that his demeanor changed.

"Here's the only issue," he declared, dropping my hand and moving toward an old and decaying tree.

"This son of a bitch can't be removed without someone takin' care of the damn beehive inside it."

I followed Billy's lead as he pointed toward a dark, hollow opening in the center of the black tree's trunk. Even in the distance, I could see the scattered flittering of countless insects. Listening closely, I could even hear the droning buzz from within, the sound of millions of diligently working bees obsessively tending to their queen.

"The contracta' I hired to build this field said these bees are some kinda' rare breed," Billy continued, reaching down for a rock as he spoke. "The kind that'll work togetha' to kill a grown man, not just sting 'em like the normal kind."

He concluded his revelation by tossing the rock at the tree. The sound of the bees amplified just seconds after the rock struck the dead bark of the trunk.

"Billy!" I screamed.

"Nah, don't worry," Billy laughed, slowly making his way back to me. "You gotta really piss 'em off for 'em to come after ya. A little rock ain't gonna do it. Ya gotta go over there and stick ya whole head in the hole or somethin'."

I shuddered at the thought.

"Billy, I don't feel very safe with this bein' out here. Billy Jr. plays out here. What if he—"

"Oh, don't worry, baby doll," Billy interrupted by cupping his hands over my face. "We've already located someone who can take care'a this. The contracta' said he should be able to get the guy out here by the end of the month. In the meantime, we just make sure that Billy Jr. doesn't wanda' past the first row of hedges."

I smiled, nodding in understanding.

"Thank ya, Billy," I whispered, slowly relaxing into the touch of his still face-cupping hands. "This field is very beautiful. I'm so hona'd ya spent all this time and money buildin' it for me."

"Well, baby girl, not so much my own time, but most certainly my money," he laughed, gently pressing his lips to my forehead. "In a month from now, my girl is gonna be out here knockin' those baseballs all the way back to Wayne County!"

I smiled and laughed with him, somehow completely calm and at ease in Billy's ongoing, seemingly genuine kindness toward me.

We spent another ten minutes or so touring the field before returning to the house. Mae was in the backyard with Billy Jr., where the young boy was tinkering around with his various toy trucks and cars.

I listened as Billy instructed Mae not to allow Billy Jr. anywhere near the field for the time being. Dutifully, Mae nodded in agreement, chirped her always cheerful and friendly "yes sir," and returned to her observation of our son.

I went to sleep that night with a new and unfamiliar feeling regarding Billy. For the first time ever, I orgasmed as he made love to me, his normal forceful thrusts and painful slamming over my body now a gentle glide and careful caress. He seemed to care about my pleasure and experience in the matter. My entire being shook and shuddered as the overwhelming climax vibrated throughout my nervous system. I didn't bother to locate my nightgown or excuse myself to the bathroom after it was finished. In an unprecedented moment of security, I relaxed into Billy's arms as he pulled me close to him, his naked body against mine both erotic and comforting as he kissed my neck and fell asleep. I listened to his breathing shift into a slower, heavier sleep mode as I re-examined the meaning of unexpected attraction to a man I had never once felt an inkling of love for. For the first time in all the years I had known Billy, I felt a spark of something greater than obliged friendship or marital servitude. For the first time in five years of marriage, I felt like this man's wife: a woman actually loved and accepted, embraced and cherished. For the first time ever, I felt whole.

"Watch me, Momma!" Billy Jr. shouted as he finally ascended the stairs to the top of the playground slide.

"I'm watchin', baby!" I called back, shadowing my eyes from the sun with both hands.

"Yay!" Mae and I cheered in unison the moment Billy Jr. touched the sand at the foot of the slide.

"They truly grow up so very fast," Mae commented as we sat side by side on the playground's sole park bench.

"That they most certainly do," I replied, keeping a watchful eye on Billy Jr. as he returned to the slide stairs for another go-round. "How're things with you and Charlie?"

I could feel Mae sinking into the bench beside me. The heat that radiated from her blushing could be felt even through the relentless fire of the afternoon sun.

"Things are well," she replied meekly, her voice lowering to a near whisper.

"So, when can I expect a weddin' invitation?"

"Oh, Mrs. Jennings!" Mae gushed, fanning herself with both hands.

"Come on now, Mae. What're ya waitin' for? Ya a wonderful woman. Ya incredible with children. You'll make the most perfect wife and motha'."

"Thank ya, Mrs. Jennings. I truly appreciate those kind words. It's just . . ."

I turned to face her after several seconds passed since her words faded into an unfinished drop.

"Mae?"

"I'm sorry, ma'am," she continued. "I just really don't know what to say. Both Charlie and myself work a lot of hours. Perhaps at some point in the future we'll be able to afford our own time and place. For now, I live with you and Mr. Jennings, and Charlie lives on the grounds of the house he oversees as groundskeepa'. There just ain't enough time or money for us to be togetha' on a full-time basis is all. But, I pray there will be someday."

I smiled and placed my hands over Mae's.

"Yes," I assured her, waiting for the young girl to raise her face to meet my eyes, "there'll be time. You'll see. You two will have plenty a'time, and plenty a'wonderful, beautiful little babies."

Mae turned away, smiling.

"And," I continued, reaching into my purse for my handkerchief, "when that time comes, if ya must leave me and little Billy Jr. here . . ."

Pulling the freshly folded white handkerchief from its neatly tucked hiding spot inside my purse, I re-clasped the bag's gold fastener and returned it to its resting place beside me on the bench.

"When that time comes, my dear friend," I continued, "I'll understand and will give my full blessin' for you and Charlie's life-long happiness togetha'."

Mae nodded and smiled at me, her brilliant-white teeth dazzling in the sun.

"Okay, Billy Jr.!" I shouted, dabbing the sweat from my brow with the handkerchief. "It's time for us to get goin'!"

I started to stand, when I heard Luke Pinder's voice.

"Judy."

I closed my eyes and refused to turn around to face him.

"Judy, please. I really need to speak with you."

"Luke, no," I answered, my words firm and strong. "We've had all the conversation I can stand. I have no interest to continue any furtha'."

"But, Judy."

I felt him touch my shoulder, my immediate response both instant and violent.

"No!" I screamed, forcefully slapping his hand away. "I've had enough a'this!"

I could feel the eyes of every single onlooker in the vicinity now focused in our direction.

"I'm gonna go fetch Billy Jr., ma'am," Mae said softly, shuffling off into the playground sand.

"Now, if you'll excuse me," I murmured.

Annoyed, I unclasped my purse and tossed the handkerchief inside without focus or care, knocking the pearl-colored leather accessory from my hand and onto the sidewalk below, the entirety of contents splashing and scattering in every possible direction.

I knelt to begin retrieving my things, when I noticed Luke doing the same.

My eyes met his as he quietly handed me the fallen purse, a collection of my personal belongings grasped tightly in the other hand.

"Thank ya," I said softly, pulling the bag from his grip and returning my focus to the rest of the mess.

"Who arranged for your brother to leave Waynesboro?" Luke asked plainly.

I continued to focus on the retrieval of the remaining purse debris, Luke assisting from his side.

"I know he couldn't have done it alone. He was in custody. Was it Sheriff?"

I continued to ignore him, brushing my knees with my free hand as I again stood to my full height.

"I just need to know how it happened, Judy," he continued, rising to his feet beside me, his height and overall presence towering over my own.

"This has nothing to do with anything official or legal," he whispered, stepping closer to me. "This is personal. I just need to know how he was able to leave Wayne County while still in custody."

"Mr. Pinder," I started, dramatically sighing to signify my annoyance, "what makes ya think I know anything about any a'that?"

I lifted my eyes to Luke's; he peered curiously back at me.

"Because he's your brother and you loved him," he replied matter-of-factly. "I refuse to believe you have just gone on and lived your life for all these years without at least trying to locate him. That, or you know where he is and are content with the way things are."

I snickered and shook my head.

"Ya just don't give up, do ya?" I sneered, my irritation rising to anger. "I've told ya time and again that I don't know where my brotha is, but ya refuse to accept that for an ansa'. I will not be disturbed by any a'this again. Now, please, stop stalkin' me each time I come into town. Anotha' encounta' like this, Mr. Pinder, and I'll have no choice but to inform my husband."

"What, so you can achieve yourself yet another beating?"

His words stunned me into an unfamiliar state of shock and near paralysis.

"How dare ya," I finally managed to reply. "How dare ya say such a thing as that to me."

"It's true, isn't it?" Luke fired back without hesitating. "It's no secret, Judy. I don't know much about you and Billy's history prior to you marrying, but I do know that he gave you his name and moved you and Francis out here to Jackson just less than a few years after the trial."

I felt my eyes flitter from the wind as I looked at Luke, his familiar, bright eyes summoning my full and complete attention.

"It's also not a secret that he mistreats you. Countless people I have spoken to have all attested to seeing or overhearing some sort of violent temper thrown your way. Hell, just a few weeks ago some of your birthday party guests recounted hearing Billy beating you upstairs while everyone was downstairs waiting for cake and gift opening."

My throat dried into a hollow, parched tube as Luke inched even closer.

"The truth about you and Billy is no secret, Judy. The whole town knows and is very willing to speak of it when asked."

"Well, shame on 'em," I finally managed to say, forcing the hair from my face that the wind repeatedly misplaced there. "And shame on ya for askin' such things."

"Judy, wait," Luke said as he gently gripped my forearm. "Let me help you. Let me help you escape all this."

My heart beat faster as I slowly turned to face him, this time ignoring the disobedience of my hair as it gave way to the whipping wind.

"I don't need ya help, Mr. Pinder," I snapped coldly. "Frankly, I'd rather die than receive anything from ya."

Luke stepped back, his eyes and head shaking in misunderstanding.

"All ya care about is you," I continued to lay into him. "Even durin' the trial. It was neva' about me. It was neva' about my pain nor sufferin'. Hell, it was neva' even about Ezra, his murda', or his family. It was always about you. Ya only cared about bein' the star a'the show, using the tragedy of the case to make ya name. No, Mr. Pinder. I want nothin' from ya. Even if what ya say is true, about my husband. Even if true, I'd rather face his wrath each and every night than ever give myself to anything you could provide. At least a strike from my husband would be authentic. Anything from you would be as contrived and pathetic as a perfectly green lawn in the desert."

Luke stepped back further, clearly struck and shocked by my revelation.

Adjusting my purse under my arm, I made one final glance at Luke's stunned and flustered expression and turned to join Mae and Billy Jr., who were waiting on the other side of the playground.

"I'm sorry, Judy," I heard Luke say as I began my trek through the uneven playground sand, my heels struggling for balance with each step.

"Is everything okay, ma'am?" Mae asked as we piled into the car, Billy's grandmother's old Ford Coupe, the vehicle he preferred me to use if and when I was given permission to leave the house. His granny had finally moved in with her son and daughter-in-law, Billy's parents, so Billy acquired the car into his vast array of collectible automobiles.

"Everything's fine, Mae. Thank ya."

I fired the Ford's ignition, tossed it in drive, and floored the accelerator, Billy Jr. and Mae's silence the evidence of my anger-fueled driving. Neither spoke until we were safely back at home and in the house.

I allowed myself an hour-long soak in the master bathroom's enormous porcelain clawfoot tub, trying my best to erase the memory and echo of Luke Pinder, both past and present.

I was nearly through, when Francis appeared in the doorway.

"How's it goin', Sista?" she asked, slowly creeping her way further into the large bathroom. "Heard ya ran into an old friend at the park today."

I moved my eyes toward the water, the disbelief that she had already heard about the encounter with Luke obvious and sprawled across my expression.

"How is the ol' Yank?"

Unsure as to how to handle this conversation, I nervously fidgeted for the bathtub's rubber plug. Forcefully yanking the chain, I relished the moment of silence the deafening groan and suction of the bath water allotted me.

Francis handed me a towel so I could stand.

"He's fine," I answered quickly. "He's just passin' through . . . wanted to say hello."

Francis peered at me curiously, her eyes slowly and carefully darting over my face.

"I see," she murmured.

"So, shall we head down for dinna'? Is Billy home yet?" I asked.

Francis glared at me coldly.

"I wouldn't know," she commented, her eyes still and icy. "He doesn't speak to me all that much anymore. Ever since you two became all lovey-dovey, he doesn't have much time for me."

I just looked at my sister, my disbelief at her selfish, one-sided comment clear and apparent.

"Well, Francis," I sighed, securing the corner of the large white bath towel under my arm. "We are husband and wife, ya know. I would think that as my sista you'd be happy to see—"

"Hell, save it, Judy," Francis shut me down. "I've stood witness to this marriage from day one, and it's always been nothin' more than a one-sided love affair. Billy loves ya, wants ya, and for whateva' reason is obsessed with ya. But you, on the otha' hand, could care less about him. I know for a fact that if it weren't for that little boy, you woulda hightailed it outta here years ago."

"Yeah, and where would that leave you, dear Sista?" I snapped back.

Francis's icy glare melted into a fiery rage.

"Ya do realize I keep him off ya?" she seethed, her lips so close to mine I could taste her breath. "He'd be beatin' and fuckin' ya far more than he does now if it wasn't for me takin' some of the pressure off ya. I do it for you, Sista. I've always been here for ya."

I couldn't help but laugh, my head tossing back as the sound escaped my lungs.

"Oh really, Francis?" I retorted, forcefully ushering my words around my broken yet continual laughter. "Ya know damn well why I married Billy in the first place. And I know damn well why it is ya insist on fuckin' my husband."

"What're ya even talkin' about?" Francis growled. "Ya married the man 'cause he offa'd to save us. With Ed gone, what were we gonna do? Starve? We're women. We'd never make it in this world on our own without a man providin' for us. So, yeah, I know damn well why ya married him. I'd have done the same."

"Okay, first of all . . ."

I paused, scanning my sister's face with silence and curiosity.

"Wait," I swallowed, nervously realizing Francis was not aware of the truth. "Ya don't know, do ya?"

She cocked her head slightly, her eyes widening in suspicion. "Know what?"

"Francis, I only married Billy 'cause I had no otha' choice."

My words seemed to strike her; she stepped back a bit, appearing to fumble for a reply.

"Billy's daddy approached me a few nights after the trial had ended. He made me a deal. If I married Billy, because Billy wanted it so badly, he'd arrange for Ed to disappear and avoid facing the consequences of his confession. With the judge declarin' a mistrial, the state was most certainly gonna retry the case, or, if Billy pled guilty, sentence him to life in prison. They couldn't do either if the suspect who had admitted to the crime just up and disappeared."

Francis gawked at me, her eyes wide and spinning.

"I thought Ed just took off."

"No," I said gently, slowly inching toward her. "He didn't wanna go. He wanted to pay the price for what he did, but I wouldn't allow him. What if they had given him the death penalty? What if they had sent him to the gas chamba', Francis? I couldn't bear that. I couldn't bear losin' yet another person I loved. So I took Billy's daddy up on his offa'. I married his son in exchange for Ed's life."

Francis fluttered her lashes, tapping her left hand over the giant marble countertop for support.

"I . . . I . . . I didn't know . . ."

"I never speak of it, Francis. How can I? I just assumed it was somethin' you had pieced togetha' on ya own."

"So all this time, that's why ya stay? Ya endure all this shit for Ed?"

"I endure all this shit for my son. Ed's been gone long enough. Whereva' he is, they haven't found him. So five years on, I stay for Billy Jr., or else, I woulda been long gone, like ya said."

Francis continued to scan my face, her eyes revealing the chaos of her mind.

"So it truly doesn't botha' ya that I fool around with ya husband?"

I smiled and shook my head.

"What kinda' fool do ya take me for, dear Francis?" I asked, lifting my hand to cup her cheek. "Do ya really think I'd allow myself the turmoil and humiliation if I really cared? I mean, come on, as ya said, ya take some of the brunt off me. He doesn't hit nor rape ya as he does me. In his own weird way, he cares about ya."

Surprisingly, a wealth of tears began to flow down my sister's face.

"No he doesn't," she sobbed, pressing her now tear-soaked skin into my palm. "He loves you."

"Francis, he—"

"I'd give anything to be you. Anything," she cried, pulling her face from my hand and locking her eyes with mine.

"He adores ya, Judy. He truly does. All he does is talk about ya. Always has. For years now. Everything is about you."

I didn't know what to say. I could only stand and listen.

"He hits ya 'cause he's frustrated. It's out of love. He wants ya to love him the way he loves you. He's told me this. Plus, I ain't blind. I see it for myself. It's as obvious as the moon in the night sky. He worships ya, Judy. Ya just don't appreciate it."

I continued to stand still, a plethora of emotion welling up behind my eyes.

"Why don't ya love him, Judy?"

"I . . . I . . ." my words fell from my mouth, clumsy and fractured.

"I see ya tryin'," Francis continued, now cupping her hand over mine. "I can see that ya wanna make things betta'."

I shook my head, tears exploding from behind my lids.

"I can't though," I cried. "I can't force it. I've tried hard for years, but I just can't."

Francis pulled me closer, both our bodies trembling through tears.

"Do ya love him?" I whispered, my voice wet and bubbled with snot and water.

Francis pulled back, her eyes absorbing the entirety of my face.

"Will it hurt ya if I say yes?"

I shook my head no.

"Then, yes. I always have. Since high school. I was always so jealous that he wanted you instead of me. I mean, come on, Judy. Between the two of us, I've always been the one who gussied up for the boys. You just neva' seemed to care, yet, the finest and most-wanted boy in all the county wanted ya. It used to kill me."

"Are ya sure it still don't?"

Francis tipped her head, her immediate expression hinting at her rage. Quickly though, I could see her force through the emotion.

"I suppose," she whispered, her expression melting into one of pain and sympathy. "I'm sorry . . ."

"Francis," I started, struggling to find the balance of my speaking voice, "I've never held this against ya. I assumed it so. It's just how it is. I don't hate ya for it. In fact, I'm grateful ya here with me.

Despite our differences, I've always found some form of comfort in havin' my one and only sista here by my side."

Francis's tears began to flow heavier.

"I love ya, Judy," she sobbed, forcing her face into my shoulder.

"I love ya too, Sista," I cooed, patting her hair with my hand.

We stood for a long moment together, our breathing slowing in unison. For the first time I could ever remember, my sister and I shared the same space, the same breath, without the chaos and anger of her rage overwhelming the situation.

"Oh my God!" Francis suddenly screamed, forcing herself out of my embrace. "The letta'!"

Her look of horror absorbed over my face. Without her uttering another word, I already understood what was happening.

"Ya gave it to Billy?"

"It's on his desk," she confirmed, her eyes wide and terrified. "Oh my God, I'm so sorry, Judy."

"Let's just go get it," I replied, moving to the closet to dress.

"He's home," she confirmed. "I saw him pull in just as I came up here. I wanted to tell ya about it before he found the . . . I'as just bein' a bitch. I wanted ya to know the wrath that was about to come ya way and why. Oh my god, Judy. I'm so sorry."

She dropped to her knees, her sobbing uncontrolled.

Panicked, I snatched my purple dressing gown from the back of the closet door and ran from the master suite. I could feel my pulse inside my throat as I neared Billy's office. The doors were closed. That was a good sign. Perhaps he had yet to go in there.

Pausing before the grand mahogany double doors, I forced myself calm and gripped one of the golden handles. Inching it open, I had a clear view of Billy's desk. Empty. He wasn't there. Thank God. In an instant, I popped into the office and began to tiptoe toward the desk. Where was the letter? I couldn't see it. The entire desk was void of paperwork. Hell, it was void of anything. It was then I realized the debris surrounding it. Every piece of paper, every lamp and bauble, every utensil and office supply was piled around the massive desk like fallen leaves below a shedding oak tree.

I froze in place, anticipating what was to come.

"Why?" I heard a voice whisper, the sound gripping my heart.

I turned to see Billy, his face blood red, his eyes stained from crying. His hair was disheveled, his tie half undone, his shirt streaked and stained with what appeared to be blood.

"Why?" he repeated, inching toward me.

"Billy, I . . . I can—"

The vision of him lunging into the air like a wildcat froze into my brain as he toppled over my body. My head slammed onto the wooden floorboards, their strength and density reverberating their force into my skull.

"Why!" he screamed, his tears and saliva showering over my skin.

He lifted the several-page letter I had written to Ms. Washington and shoved it over my face. I couldn't breathe as the paper began to dampen from Billy's tears, sealing over my mouth and nose like plaster.

Just as I started to feel myself fade into blackness, he snatched the paper away and lifted me into his arms. I wasn't fully aware of anything, when he tossed my body onto his massive desk and lunged over me.

"I've given ya everything!" he bellowed. "Everything!"

He started to fumble with the silk belt of my robe. Before I could react, he spread it open and pinned my arms down. With his free hand, I could hear him undoing his pants.

"Billy, please . . . I—"

Blackness. His fist pummeled into the side of my skull, sturdy and forceful. Several seconds passed before I could open my eyes. I felt him tear into my flesh just as I was able to blink, the vision of Billy's beet-red face filling my entire field of vision.

"Fuckin' nigga-lovin' whore!" he screamed, thrusting his pelvis with force and rage against my hips. "Fuckin' whore!"

The world began to spin, my senses dulling to meek embers. I could feel myself begin to numb and dissipate into unconsciousness, when the sound of another voice filled the echo.

"Billy, stop!" I heard Francis scream.

I opened my eyes to see Billy snatch his head behind him, his voice muffled and angry in the distance.

"Get the fuck outta here, Francis!" I could hear him yell, the sound of his voice as far off as the sun.

Slowly, I reentered my body, every press of Billy's skin and thrust of his hips heightened throughout my being. Summoning every bit of strength I could muster, I pulled my right knee toward my chest and launched it at Billy's groin. I could feel the hair of his manhood beneath my toes as I forced him from on top of me. He disappeared from my sight, the sound of his body toppling from the desk echoing in the slight distance.

Scrambling, I gathered my robe and fastened the silk belt around me, crouching into a crawl-like position and leaping from the desk. I burst through the giant french doors that lined the back wall of Billy's office, and dashed into the backyard.

I didn't turn around when I heard Billy's voice call after me, the sound of his running inching up from behind. I ran and ran, the dividing line of hedges that separated the backyard from the open fields coming into view. In the distance, I could see the baseball field, the lifeless, black tree towering over it.

"Judy!" Billy screamed, his voice so harsh and loud I could sense pain in my throat just from the sound of it.

I ran, thorns and rocks slicing into the bottom of my bare feet.

I was just entering the baseball field, when Billy tackled me.

I struggled to break free of his grip, but he was simply far too strong.

"I thought things was betta'!" he screamed, his voice high and almost childlike. "I thought you was happia!'"

He flipped me onto my back and started to unfasten my belt again. Rearing up, I lunged both legs at his hips, knocking him from his kneed stance and onto the ground. I closed the robe and jumped to my feet. I was just starting to run, when Billy grabbed my ankle, pulling me back to the dirt. My breath escaped as my stomach slammed onto the hard earth.

"How could ya write that letta'?" Billy yelled, though we were only inches apart. "Ya don't love me at all!"

"Billy, wait—"

I felt him kick me, his entire body now towering above.

"There ain't nothin' left for ya to say, whore! Ya done said it all in ya letta'!"

I started to choke as clumps of grass and red dirt funneled into my nose and mouth.

"Ya said ya loved me! That's a lie! I've always known it! Ya just tolerate me! Ya've only ever loved that nigga!"

"Please, Billy, I—"

"I only wanted to give ya everything, Judy!"

His voice was so raw and powerful that I could hear the bees in the nearby tree groan and bellow.

"I even killed for ya!"

The world froze around me. My brain was now consumed by Billy's voice.

"Ya know damn well Ed didn't do it! Sure, he beat the shit outta that boy, but he didn't kill him!"

Billy didn't interfere as I lifted myself from the ground without thought or effort. Before I knew it, we stood face-to-face. An eternity of seconds passed before Billy spoke again. His demeanor was now calm and controlled.

"Truth is," he started, his voice relaxed and eerily gleeful, "ya right about everything ya accused me of the otha' night. It was me who got ya in the woods that night, Judy. And, yeah, ya nigga boyfriend did try and stop me, and that's why I brought all hell down on him. But those boys wasn't gonna kill him . . . Ed and the Bensons. They just wanted to scare him a bit. But I was there, Judy. I carried ya to ya house after I chased that boy off. I told Ed how I saved ya. Ya shoulda' seen how ya brotha cried like a baby at the sight of ya, all bloody and black and blue. Afta' Ed rushed ya to the hospital, he rounded up Fred and Ron and headed out to find the boy. I waited at the Benson farm while they searched. That's why none of them colored witnesses ever saw me. I ain't no fool. I know how it all works. Later on, I even got my granny to lie to that bastard Yankee, sayin' that durin' the time ya brotha and them was off huntin' for the boy, I was with her at her house, where she was tendin' to my wounds . . . the wounds I had suffa'd durin' the heroic endeva' that surely saved ya life. A betta' attorney woulda been suspicious of my story and interrogated me furtha', especially on the witness stand. That's why I refused to testify. That Yankee figya'd I' as just tryin' to protect ya brotha and them, 'specially when my story didn't line up with Ed's testimony that it was me who told Ed that it was ya nigga boyfriend who attacked ya. That would'a hurt the Yank's narrative for the motive, so he just left me outta it. Jim Hemming didn't care enough to have me testify. He knew he had the whole damn thing in the bag from the start. I shoulda been a suspect though. But, like with everyone, that Yankee trusted my alibi simply because'a who I am. But that whole trial was a joke. Ya brotha was a fuckin' fool for takin' the blame. That Yankee was neva' gonna prove a damn thing with a headless body as his only evidence. Maybe Ed just felt guilty for bearin' witness to what I'd done, or maybe it was all the newspapa' reporta's and such that had him scared. Even still, despite all that, those good ol' boys on that jury was neva' gonna convict a white man, much less three of 'em. 'Specially when they was just out rightin' a sinful wrong committed against a white woman. Still, it all worked out in the end. Ed made it easy for me. My daddy sure didn't want to, but I threatened to never speak to him again unless he approached ya with that deal to save ya brotha. I knew it was the only way I could eva' get ya to marry me. My daddy sure as hell put his whole career on the line for that, but it got me what I wanted."

Billy paused, allowing his unexpected revelation to absorb into my brain.

"There ain't nothin' gonna keep me from ya, Judy. I killed for ya once, and I'll kill for ya again."

The wind swirled around us, the sound of an approaching thunderstorm rumbling in the distance.

"I cut that nigga boy's head clean off with my own two hands."

His emotionless admission of guilt arrowed right through the very core of my soul. I could feel streams of hot tears soaking down my face, my heart struggling to find a steady rhythm.

"Ed did try and stop me, but I made those Benson boys hold him back as I sliced right through that nigga's throat and sawed right through to the other side. I ain't never seen so much blood in all my life. It was everywhere. On all a'us. Ed and the boys got scared, but not me. No, I stayed steady. I wrapped that head up in a burlap sack and buried it out in the woods behind the Benson place. Ed held a kerosene lamp while I did it. Meanwhile, the Benson boys took the body down to the deep part of a creek that ran through the edge of their property. Damn fools barely weighed it down, so it's no wonda' it washed up just a few weeks lata'. But I knew what I'as doin'. Hell, I even buried my bloody clothes and the huntin' knife I'd used under the floorboards of my granny's basement. They ain't never gonna be found there. Had Ed not let guilt get the best a'him, that head would'a neva' been found eitha'."

He paused again, this time a slight glint of what appeared to be joy, perhaps even jubilation, tugging at the corner of his half smile.

"No, Judy. I took ya nigga boyfriend out and got away with it. I'll do the same with our son."

My heart froze as I suddenly realized the source of blood that was splashed over Billy's button-down shirt.

"What did ya do?" I questioned in a semi-whisper, my voice hoarse and broken with shock and a multitude of emotions. "What did ya do to Billy Jr.?"

"He's the only one ya really care about 'round here," he growled, his fists clenched, his mouth gnarled. "Ya don't give a fuck about me."

"What did ya do to my son!" I cried, stepping toward him.

"Our son!" he screamed, raising a fist to my face. "He's our son!"

He stepped back, lowering both arms to his side. I watched as he stumbled backward and fell to his knees.

I leapt at Billy, kicking him in the chest as I screamed.

"Where is he!"

Billy lifted himself from the red dirt, where my kick had knocked him from his knees. He grinned, his eyes wild and dark, his hair whipping from the force of the wind as the angry weather drew closer.

"I knocked his ass out, Judy," he cackled. "I ain't never gonna let anyone stand between you and me. Not some smooth-talkin' nigga, and certainly not some snot-faced little kid."

He inched closer, the reflection of my face in the blackness of his eyes as clear and detailed as a freshly developed photograph.

"Ya all mine, Judy. Always have been. Always will be."

I started to lunge toward him again, but he kicked me to the ground. I struggled to stand as he pressed his shoe into the center of my back.

"The boy ain't dead yet, Judy, but he will be. Ya think I can't make him disappear? Hell, I could bury him and that nigga maid in the storm cellar and just tell everyone she done ran off with him, and no one would even question it. Ya brotha and those boys nearly went down for what I did back in Waynesboro. I can always shift the blame. Hell, I fuckin' control it. I'll always get away with it. I'm too damn smart and too damn connected to ever go down for anything."

I couldn't move under the pressured force of his shoe over my back. I inched and wriggled, but could only manage to suck in more red dirt and grass.

"Ya brought this on, Judy," Billy continued, lowering his head toward the ground so I could hear him better. "I never liked the kid anyway. Too whiny. Too much like a girl."

He laughed to himself, pressing his foot harder into my spine.

"Too much like his momma."

I felt him ease off, stepping back so I could move.

"I'll make sure it's quick. Don't worry. I at least care enough about the little brat to not let him suffa'."

I sprung to my feet, swatting at Billy with both fists.

"It's too late, whore!" he growled, catching both of my arms with one hand. "Ya done laid it all out in ya letta'. Ya said ya truth. This the way it's gotta be, girl. Ya won't love me, so I'll take away everything in ya life ya love till there ain't nothin' or no one left but me."

A demon-like grin shadowed his face as he inched closer.

"Hell, even God himself murda'd his own Son for love. A love he demands from the world through fear. As with God, Judy, you will love me or suffer hell itself."

He shoved me to the ground and started to walk off the field.

Jumping to my feet, I ran and clamped onto his back like a wild animal. Without much effort, he gripped both of my wrists, pulled me from his body, and swung me toward the tree.

"Go on, girl! Keep it up! Rile them bees up! See what it's like when they take a likin' to ya ass!"

It was then that I saw it: the ax, its blade gleaming in the dim light, streaks of lighting reflecting over its wide-open face. It was lodged in the side of the tree, where it was ready and waiting to remove the decaying trunk once the bees had safely been eliminated. The near white of the wooden handle juxtaposed the blacked bark like the arm of a skeleton.

I rolled toward it, avoiding Billy's legs as he towered above me.

Crawling up the side of the tree trunk, I felt several bees torpedo into my hair and onto the sides of my face. Instantly, they began to sting me, their rage and anger as thundering as the fast-approaching storm. Without hesitation, I fell onto the handle of the ax, using it to lift myself into a full stance.

"Whatcha gonna do, girl?" I heard Billy laugh. "Ya really think I'm gonna let ya get that ax outta that tree?"

I turned to face him, a black curtain of rain accenting the background behind him.

"I'm gonna drag ya ass back inside that house and make ya watch me kill that little boy."

Thunder. Lighting.

"Hell, maybe I'll even bring that ax along. I'm sure it'll make takin' that lil' boy's head off a lot easier than that huntin' knife did with ol' Ezra."

The moment Billy uttered Ezra's name, the handle of the ax released from the tree and into my grasp.

"Step over, Miss Judy-Bee," I heard Ezra say, his voice clear and audible even in the chaos of the wind. "Keep ya eye on the ball and knock it outta here."

There wasn't much more than a crack as I swung the ax as fast and furiously as any baseball bat I had ever held. I saw Billy's body topple onto the tree, the swarming bees flooding over it as quickly as it landed.

I didn't see his head, nor did I look. I ran with all my might as fast as I could toward the house, the reverberating thunder clapping behind each streak of lighting the very second it veined across the sky.

"Where's Billy Jr.!" I shrieked as I pummeled through the french doors of the living room.

There was no one there.

"Mae! Francis!"

My voice was higher and shriller than I had ever heard it, my fear and trauma as evident as the outside thunderstorm.

"Billy Jr.!"

I entered the kitchen to see both my sister and Mae on their knees, a bleeding Billy Jr. lying in a pool of blood before them.

"No!" I bellowed, so loud that my ears rang from the echo.

I fell onto my son, his blood mixing with his father's, which was still smeared and splattered all over my face.

I could feel Mae and Francis gripping me, their voices hollow and echoed beneath the deafening ring of my ears. I pulled the boy into my arms, his head dropping back, but his little body trembling and breathing.

"Oh, thank God," I whispered, lifting his face and pressing it against my own.

It was then that someone pulled the boy from my arms and lifted him into the air. It was several seconds before I could make out the image of Charlie, Mae's boyfriend, handing my son over to a team of paramedics.

In a dreamlike haze, the vision of the paramedics, police officers, and other various figures filled the space around my head as I felt myself falling into blackness. I saw them close my son into an ambulance, his eyes open, his tiny voice crying out my name.

"He's alive," I said aloud. "Thank God Almighty, my boy's alive!"

Part III

Mississippi State Penitentiary
1963

8

The Books

T he clicking of the cell door jolted me awake. I didn't resist as two male guards shackled my ankles and wrists. As the sole female prisoner at Mississippi State Penitentiary, I was kept isolated in a maximum-security cell, completely separate from the rest of the prison population. Fears of attacks, both physical and sexual, limited my access to any of the traditional recreational activities most of the other prisoners were privy to. Shockingly, the all-male guard staff never once tried to take advantage of my womanhood or female vulnerabilities. Nearing the one-year anniversary of my imprisonment here, I had nothing but praise and respect for the prison staff. Perhaps their compassion was due to the constant eye of the warden, the unrelenting curiosity of the media, or maybe even a tinge of sympathy and understanding toward my circumstances.

The sound of my chains echoed around the corridor. I followed the guards down the familiar path to the visitors' room. I had yet another meeting with Luke Pinder, a man who had become a source of stability and strength for me throughout my trial and subsequent conviction.

The jury had found me guilty. The sentence, unanimous: death. The media fervor surrounding my trial had rivaled that of the one for Ezra's murder. The headlines wrote themselves: The surviving victim of an apparent Negro attack marries the Mississippi attorney general's son, bears his only child, beheads husband five years later. Regardless of the now-verified details of Billy's confession to me the night he died—the heap of bloody clothes and massive blood-stained hunting knife buried beneath the floorboards of his granny's basement—the prosecution still drilled home the fact that I had ruthlessly decapitated—murdered—my husband, the father of my child, and the son of the state's chief legal officer and former prominent Wayne County citizen. Attorney General Jennings retired after my trial, the shame and embarrassment over the actions of his now-deceased son far too gruesome and heady to bear. After the bloody clothes and hunting knife were unearthed from the basement, Mr. Jennings sold his Waynesboro boyhood home, the oversized Jennings family house, which Elie Jennings had left to her son after her passing, and resettled with his wife somewhere in Florida. In an act of unselfish and perhaps guilt-motivated kindness, Mr. Jennings paid off the rest of the mortgage on the plantation house, agreeing to allow Francis, Billy Jr., Mae, and her now-husband, Charlie, to remain living there. With the house now paid for, the three adult residents operated it as a bed and breakfast, the lurid details of the on-site murder either attracting or dispelling the clientele.

Luke Pinder oversaw the legal adoption of Billy Jr. to Francis. Aside from Luke, Francis had become my greatest source of love and support. She visited me weekly, daily if it were allowed, always doing her best to distract me from my grim reality with either the presence of my son, pictures of him, or updates and general gossip about the goings-on of the Jackson elite.

None of the people I had once considered as friends, or at the very least, acquaintances—Billy's lawyer friends and their wives nor the neighbors of the plantation house—ever bothered to visit or even contact me. I was now a bona fide outcast; once a tolerated pariah, now a shameful curse. Many gave exaggerated or downright false accounts to the press, insinuating or flatly accusing me of being an unfaithful wife, a raging alcoholic, or worst of all, an unfit and abusive mother. The fabricated tall tales that decorated the nation's headlines had once crippled my will to live. I had spent months barely eating, curled atop my moldy prison mattress, weeping until my eyes were completely devoid of tears. It was Luke and Francis who got me through. Their constant visits and cheerful disposition were not only a warm and welcome distraction, but also an outright necessity for my emotional stability and well-being.

Although he now practiced law as a private attorney, Luke had not been my defense attorney during the trial. Despite having been married to the attorney general of Mississippi's defense attorney son, or perhaps because of it, I was delegated a fresh-out-of-school defense attorney who knew as much about law as I did. He at least knew enough to recommend that I plead guilty to the first-degree murder charge in order to avoid a trial, the likelihood of my sentence being life imprisonment over the death penalty highly probable. I refused though, for I believed any level-headed jury would have seen Billy's threat on the life of our son as maternal protection. Instead, I was painted as a revenge-thirsty, scorned wife, the years of betrayal, infidelity, and physical abuse finally forcing me to my breaking point. The prosecution had several witnesses testify to observing some form of abuse, verbal or physical, from Billy toward me. They used this testimony to secure a motive. The threat on Billy Jr.'s life was seen as no more than a feeble excuse for the dignity-ravaged wife, who had lured her overbearing and abusive husband out to the baseball field with the plan to decapitate him premeditated and cruelly executed.

The state pressed hard not only to have me suffer the consequences of committing such a brutal and inhumane act, but also to perhaps avenge and even-out some sort of unseen dues regarding the embarrassing and still shameful Ezra Washington murder trial. No one ever said it, but I felt as though I were somehow paying the price for the state's, namely Luke's, incompetence during that first trial. In an ironic twist, here was the assistant district attorney, now private attorney, from that failed trial doing everything in his power to help save my life. Working with a team of other pro bono lawyers, my sentence was appealed, but my conviction and sentence affirmed.

Francis did what little she could to help fund the new defense team, but despite living in a Mississippi mansion, her personal funds were limited at best. Billy's father had been kind enough to pay off the house, but the bulk of Billy's fortune—cars, jewelry, and expensive clothing—had all been either reclaimed by the family, sold, or auctioned. In the end, Francis and I had nothing. We were as poor and nearly broke as we had been when Billy first took us from our Waynesboro cottage.

"Hey, beautiful." Luke smiled as I was placed in the chair across from him. "How you holding up?"

"Oh, just swimmingly, sir." I smirked. "The service at this spa is simply divine."

We laughed together, a brief, subtle escape from the hellish monotony of incarceration.

"How you doing with the manuscript?" Luke asked, nervously fumbling with his briefcase.

"Fine," I answered, watching his hands twist and fumble over the large, oversized leather case. "Why? What's wrong?"

Luke paused and slowly lifted his eyes.

"It's just me now, Judy."

I showed no emotion as I responded to him.

"The otha' attorneys quit?"

"The other attorneys have no faith. They quit. Yes."

I watched as Luke returned to fumbling his briefcase.

"Is there a date?"

My question stopped him cold.

"Luke?" I prompted when he failed to respond. "Have they set an execution date?"

"Judy . . . I think we need to—"

"Just answer me, Luke, please."

I looked on as tears began to fill Luke Pinder's eyes and escape down his cheeks. I knew there was a date before he ever even opened his mouth.

"November 30th," he eventually answered, his tears glowing under the overhead fluorescents. "Judy, there's still a chance—there's still hope we can appeal to—"

"November 30th," I repeated, stopping his flow of panicked words. "That'll be enough time. I'll be finished before then."

Luke peered at me helplessly, his face filled with heavy and extreme defeat and sorrow.

"I'm so sorry, Judy," he whispered, tears flipping from his lips. "We tried, I swear. The state just wants this taken care of and moved out of the headlines. You confessed, Judy. There isn't a way we can argue an unfair trial or some sort of mistake with the investigation or prosecution. You gave them exactly what was needed when you detailed everything so vividly. Hell, you might as well have had the whole thing filmed and delivered straight to the jury. We can still go beyond the state level though. I'll work for you forever. Please, let's just—"

I placed my shackled hands over Luke's forearms, locking my eyes over his.

"It's fine, Luke," I whispered. "No more appeals. Let's just do what needs to be done."

I could feel him welling with more words of misguided hope and bargaining, but he resisted. Instead, we simply looked at one another for what felt like an entire lifetime.

"Is the deal still on?" I finally asked, breaking the much-needed silence. "Will they still publish?"

"Yes, of course," Luke replied, darting his eyes over my face. "This book will be huge, Judy. The entire world is waiting to hear your side of the story. From everything with Ezra, to your marriage to Billy. The murder."

He moved his eyes nervously around the room, the scattered guards eyeing him in return.

"I have everything set up. All the proceeds will go directly to Billy Jr.'s trust. Francis will be allotted a support allowance until Billy Jr. is eighteen."

"Perfect," I smiled, nodding my head in approval.

"Five!" one of the guards called, signaling the end of the visitor period.

"Judy," Luke whispered, reaching for my hand, "there's something else."

I eyed him nervously, suddenly fearful of what he was about to reveal.

"There's someone who wants to see you," he continued, nervously fidgeting his fingers over my open palms. "I can't tell you much more. Just be ready to see someone in perhaps a week or so. Whatever information I give to you prior will have to be strictly adhered to. Beforehand and during. Do you understand?"

I nodded in uncertain agreement, but had no time to question Luke further. The two guards lifted me from the chair and pulled me toward the door.

"I'll see you next week, Judy," Luke called as I was marched from the room. "Stay strong. I love you."

I spent the next several days doing nothing but writing. I had started the project just after my arrest, which was a few weeks before my trial, and well before I knew of my sentence to die. I started at the beginning, from the day I had first met Ezra in high school, all the way through to that fateful day on the backyard baseball field.

I didn't think much about what had happened on that day. Rumor had it, Billy's head had been found in the woods far beyond the property line. They say the ax had removed his head with such clean precision that even the finest doctor or Medieval executioner would be envious. I didn't know if any of that were true; I never saw much more than Billy's body slump into the tree, nor did I care about the lurid details. In my heart, I had saved my son's life. Of course, in a roundabout way, I had also avenged Ezra's death. But on that day, in that moment, my only thought was of Billy Jr. I didn't know for certain if Billy would have lived up to his threat. I could never imagine that he would actually murder our son right in front of me, but how could I chance it? How could I risk not stopping the man who had just boldly and explicitly detailed to me the gruesome details of a murder he had committed with his own two hands? Ironically, it was a beheading that had stopped him; a sinister yet befitting twist of fate only the hand of God himself could orchestrate.

Tears stained the notebook as I recounted the horrors of the rape, now known to be perpetrated by Billy, all the way through a retelling of the subsequent trial and the last time I had seen my brother, Ed. I wondered aloud throughout the completely filled notebook as to where my brother was. Where he lived now. What he knew and didn't know. How his life had progressed and changed. Who he was or who he shared his life with. One of the hardest aspects of accepting my fate was the haunting notion that I may very well go to my grave without ever knowing what had become of my beloved brother. I cited this several times throughout the pages, my heart and wounded soul laid bare throughout the scrawled narrative of the two-hundred-page notebook, each page filled front and back.

Nothing though, absolutely nothing, could ever come close to comparing to the absolute and inescapable agony I felt over the loss of my son. Sure, he was still alive to breathe the fresh air, run the fields behind the plantation house, enjoy Mae's homecooked meals, even participate in his Aunt Francis's constant attentiveness and interactions, but he was no longer mine. He was no longer with me or at my side. I had asked Francis to stop bringing him with her on her visits, mostly because of the pain and misunderstanding I could see in the young boy's face. His daddy was gone, his mommy locked inside some scary, strange building, yet he had no way to comprehend or fully understand why. Francis did her best to both console and inform him of the situation, and I appreciated her efforts, but I no longer felt it was healthy or necessary for my son to continue seeing me this way. In a completely separate notebook, I had been scrawling my seemingly endless love letter to my son. It was what I wanted to leave with him, not the memories of a shackled and defeated woman. As I carefully read over and touched up my main manuscript, I ended each evening with several-page-long entries into the notebook for Billy Jr. Not only did I recount for him the memories of our first five years together, memories I knew the maturing of his brain would soon discard, but I also ensured my limitless love for him, both now and into the beyond. I promised to always be with him, however that was. I promised to watch his happiness and success in life unfold and manifest in whatever ways his heart saw fit. I promised to always cherish his presence, even after my heart ceased to beat and my lungs failed to breathe. For my son, I promised him a love that would truly last forever.

Exactly one week later, both books were completed: the manuscript and the journal for Billy Jr. I wrapped them each in brown paper, watching as one of the guards carefully tied a string around both. On the cover of one: *For Billy Jr.,* the other: *His Name Was Ezra.*

9

Sergeant Thomas

It's wonderful, Judy. It really is," Luke remarked some three weeks later, after having read the manuscript. As promised, the journal to Billy Jr. was sent to Francis, who had agreed to keep it wrapped and sealed until she felt Billy Jr. was old enough to understand it.

"The only thing is," Luke continued, nervously tapping his fingers on the small metallic table between us, "you're incredibly explicit regarding your feelings of love and passion for Ezra. That may be off-putting to some readers."

"Why?" I asked, adjusting myself in my chair, the rattling of my chains clanking and smacking the metal seat. "It's the truth. It's how I feel. Why should that be a turn-off?"

"Well, Judy," Luke said, nervously darting his eyes from the tabletop to my face, "times are changing, yes. I mean, so much is happening right now with our country. The Civil Rights Movement, Martin Luther King Jr., outlawing Jim Crow . . . but even still, people have their prejudices regarding interracial couples. Even those who support equal rights for blacks still have issues with race mixing and whatnot. I just think it may be a bit much. Perhaps you should consider toning it down a bit."

"Luke," I said, reaching my shackled hands toward him, "if I change one word of my story, if I censor or cut anything out that is real or true . . . then none of it matta's. This book won't matta'. My life . . . my death."

Luke stared, his face searching for an expression.

"Don't ya think I'm sittin' here right now because I had the gall to love a black man?"

My words seemed to strike him like a stone.

"I mean, come on, Luke, let's be honest. The murmurs and rumors. The way people scoffed and mocked me, usually behind my back, in Waynesboro. Years later, in Jackson, it was the same. They pitied Billy for marryin' the 'nigga lova'.' They didn't think I deserved to be with a man of Billy's stature. They felt he deserved better. No, Luke. The fact that I sit here before ya now on death row is exactly where many feel I should've always been. To them, it didn't take me killin' a white man to put me here. The fact that I had the courage to love a black man in the face of their racism was enough to send me to the gas chamba'. Those people will never see what I did to Billy as a form of self-defense, for myself or the life of my son, nor will they see it as justice for what Billy did to Ezra. In the end, to many, I'm broken goods. A torn, tattered flowa' sullied and dirtied by the hands of a Negro man. My sentence to die is a way to not only punish me or right some racial wrong in their minds, but to erase me. Diminish me. Extinguish me."

Luke continued to stare, my face reflected in the water of his eyes.

"So, my story must be accurate and true. Raw and unfiltered. For anything else would not only be a disservice to myself, but also a disservice to Ezra's memory, his family, and to everyone who has ever had the strength to follow their heart, regardless of where it led 'em, and despite those who told 'em it was wrong."

Luke nodded, his face expressing a definite understanding.

"I get it," he whispered, still nodding. "I truly get it."

"When they strap me in that chair inside that gas chamba'," I started, my voice strong and certain, "I want 'em to know, his name was Ezra . . . not just some hateful word like 'black boy,' 'Negro' . . . or 'nigga.' He was a man. A kind, gentle, lovin' man. And I loved him. Despite what anyone said or did . . . I loved him . . . and I still love him. No one can take or remove that from me. They can try, but they can't steal his memory away. Not here, not in that chamba', and not in whatever lies beyond."

I gripped my hands over Luke's.

"This book will ensure that his memory lives on foreva'. The injustice of his death will live in infamy. Years from now, long afta' I'm gone . . . long afta' you are gone, people will rememba' this story, and the first words out of their mouths will be, 'His name was Ezra.'"

"Okay," Luke whispered, moving his hands out from under mine and placing them on top of my fingers. "You're right. Nothing needs to change. It's perfect."

I smiled.

"Now," Luke's voice deepened, detailing the serious tone of what he was about to reveal, "I don't know how else to tell you or prepare you for this without just coming straight out and saying it."

He adjusted himself in his chair, his eyes darting nervously over each of the guards.

"I found your brother. Back when I was still a DA, I hired a private investigator to search for both your brother and the Bensons. He finally tracked Ed down just a month or so after your arrest. He was on a military base. He had a completely different name, birth certificate, you name it. However he managed it, I don't know, but he was never gonna be found without an ongoing fight. Anyway, I kept the file. Honestly, I was still gonna press the matter and force the state to go after him, but once your trial began and it became known that Billy had confessed to Ezra's murder . . . not only did my pursuance of Ed become irrelevant, but it felt wrong. I had always dreamed of one day finding Ed and pursuing and winning a retrial. I knew finding the man who had disappeared after confessing to a murder, especially a nationally famous, racially charged murder, would not only make my career, it'd make me a star. Hell, I wanted nothing else more in the entire world."

He leaned forward in his chair, a hint of tears lining his lower lids.

"You were right about me, Judy. I had been using you because of your brother. It stopped being about Ezra or his family . . . or even you. It became all about me, my life, my career . . . my fame. Then, one day, it all hit me. Justice had already been served. You served it. In the end, pursuing Ed just didn't matter anymore. Sure, one could say it was the fact that Billy confessed to you that changed everything, but it was much more than that. It woke me up. This wasn't about Ed, or even you . . . this was about humanity. All of us. Truth, life, and justice for us all."

My head was spinning in disbelief. I couldn't even form words to respond with.

"So, I kept the file. He's been locked on the base for several years. He had no idea you had married Billy, and certainly no clue about the whole ordeal and trial. It wasn't easy, but I managed to contact him. He is now aware of everything and is on his way to see you. Thing is . . . we have to keep his identity a secret. He's established himself a pretty admirable military career, and if the truth is known that he was once a suspected murderer and a runaway felon, well . . . at this point, I just don't think it'd be right to take all that away from him."

Shock and disbelief still locked the use of my voice. I could hardly breathe.

"So please, don't make this about anything more than what it is. He's your brother and he wants to see you."

"Five!" the guard shouted, signaling the final five minutes of the visitor session.

"He goes by Sergeant Thomas now," Luke continued, lowering his voice until it was barely audible. "Please, only refer to him as such. We're taking a huge risk by bringing him not only back to Mississippi, but also into such a highly guarded and visitor-scrutinized setting. Not to mention, the nosey reporters who still clamor outside. Please, Judy. You've got to prepare yourself to interact with him as if he weren't your brother . . . as if he isn't someone you haven't seen in years. You have to play it safe."

I didn't respond as I was lifted from the chair and led to the doorway.

"Next week, Judy," Luke called from behind me. "Be prepared for next week."

I spent nearly every waking hour of the entire next week shuffling through my mind and feelings regarding how I felt about seeing Ed. On one hand, I was desperate to face him, to see him, touch him, feel his familiar, warm presence. On the other, I struggled with the image of him being present as Billy took the hunting knife to Ezra's neck. Although Billy had confessed to me that Ed had tried to stop him from killing Ezra, but Billy had the Benson boys hold him back, why didn't he tell on Billy? Why did he take the blame for the entire murder? Why was he trying to protect the one who was actually guilty?

The questions continued to swirl and dominate my brain until the very second I saw him. Ed, my only brother, tall and handsome in his uniform, his face beautiful and clean-shaven beneath his hat.

My heart froze as he took the seat across from me, the memories of a million hours spent together reflooding my heart.

"Hello, Ms. Bracewell," he said sternly, the guards retreating to their allotted corners of the room. "I'm here to discuss an interview piece for our military journal."

I cleared my throat and forced my voice to speak.

"Uh, yes, Sergeant. That's fine."

He lowered his head and leaned forward, his eyes locked on mine, but his brain scanning the guards with his peripheral vision. Once settled, he whispered, "Judy . . ."

Tears instantly brimmed my lower lids. It took every single ounce of self-control I could muster not to break down.

"Ed," I whispered back, resisting the urge to move my hands toward him across the tiny metallic table.

"I have some interview questions I'd like for ya to look ova' and ansa' at ya leisure. Ya can return it to me via the accompanyin' self-addressed and postage-marked envelope."

I nodded, taking the folded paper as he slid it over the tabletop.

Remarkably, none of the guards seemed to notice. Prison protocol forbade any sort of exchange during the visitor sessions. Any letters or mail had to be filtered and processed through the prison office, each and every document opened, read, and scrutinized. I realized there was something here Ed didn't want anyone else to read.

We spent the next fifteen minutes discussing American politics, racial divide, the Civil Rights Movement, as well as the impending Vietnam War.

"The nation is ready if needed," Ed warned, signaling his belief that the United States would indeed enter the ongoing, controversial conflict.

It took every bit of me to not lunge for my brother, to embrace and touch him one last time. I couldn't prove it, but I could sense that it was the same for him.

He stood as the guards lifted me from my chair and marched me from the room. With one final glance over my shoulder, I saw a single tear streaming down my brother's face as he watched them guide me out the door.

November 3, 1963

Judy,

God answered my prayer. I've wanted nothing more in my entire life than to somehow see or speak to you again. After I left Waynesboro, I spent nearly a year living in basements, barns, storm cellars, you name it. I have to give it to Mr. Jennings. He kept his word, and over time, he was able to provide me an entire new identity. Birth certificate, name, birthdate, IDs. This allowed me to work and eventually join the army. This changed everything for me. I feel like I was made to do this, to serve and protect our country. To sacrifice and do what is right. I feel it is the very least I can do with my life.

It haunts me, Judy. Every time I close my eyes or allow my mind to wander, even years on. If only I could go back to that night and do something differently. If only I could go back and make some different choices. I can still see him there, beaten from my fists, scared, terrified, yet somehow strong. He stood in the face of our hatred and never allowed his integrity, soul, or character to degrade or lower to our level. I swear to you, Sister, I never wanted that boy to die. When Billy told me that Ezra had attacked you, I did what any good brother would have done. I protected my sister. I righted a wrong. I sought justice. It didn't matter about race or color or anything like that. It all became about family, love, and protection. Sure, I beat the hell out of him. Something I am not proud of. But that was all I wanted to do. I'm not sure where I went or what happened to me when I saw Billy pull that hunting knife. It all happened so fast. I swear, I thought he was only going to threaten the boy with it. I never imagined he was actually going to use it on him. The image replays in my mind like an old filmstrip stuck on the reel. There wasn't a sound. No screams, no cries. Hearing now that Billy confessed to you that he was the one who hurt you in the woods and that Ezra was trying to save you makes it all that much clearer now. Knowing what I know now, I can honestly say, if there is anything to be said of stoic or heroic deaths, this would most certainly be one of them. Looking back, it's obvious Billy knew what he was doing from the very start. He knew he was going to set it up so me and the Bensons would take the fall for what he did. He was smart. Not to mention, he was the attorney general's son. Even though, at the time, I still believed it was Ezra who had hurt you, I just felt that taking the blame was the right thing to do. Someone needed to. It had gone too far. Someone needed to pay the price for that boy's death. In the end, my hands were as bloody as Billy's. Sure, I didn't hold the knife, but I also didn't stop it. I witnessed a life drain from this earth far before its time.

Despite what you may believe about me, Judy, I never had an issue with the way you felt for Ezra. I know it just isn't the way things are done where we come from, but I am wise enough to know how the heart works. It doesn't see race, nor age, nor anything limited. It's about the soul. It's about something greater than ourselves. I mourn that loss for you, Judy. I mourn for having had a hand in destroying it from your life. If there was ever a way where I could fully say I was sorry, I would go to the ends of the earth to do it. But I know one can never go back. I can't change the past. I can only try to improve the future. Both for myself and my fellow man.

I wish I had been there the very first time Billy ever laid a hand on you. Luke gave me the court transcripts. I read every word. I swear, I clenched my fists so tight my palms bled from the slice of my fingernails. Those years of abuse . . . if I could ever go back and change that, my God, how I would. I'm so sorry,

Judy. Sorry for letting you down. Sorry for taking away someone you loved. And sorry for not being there for you when you
needed me most. If it means anything at all, I promise to spend
the rest of my life, be it long or short, fighting for what is right
in this world. Fighting for equality and justice. Fighting for the
right for one person to openly and freely love whoever it is their
heart sees fit.

I love you, my sister. It's all I can do not to try to break into
that prison and take you out of there. In time, if it's safe, I'll
reach out to Francis and your son. For the time being, the iron is
still too hot, and I must remain fastened to the new identity I've
created for myself. I'm sure I'll have to answer to the Almighty
when my time comes. Until that day, I'll fight. I'll do what's
right. I'll lay down my life for peace.

It is my heart's greatest prayer that you will someday forgive
me. Be it here on this earth or in heaven. Please know, I have never
not loved you, Sister. From the day Daddy died to that moment
Momma walked out the door, I saw it as my sole duty to love and
protect you and Francis. Perhaps I did it wrong, but please know
that my heart was always in the right place. I love you to the
moon and back, Judy. May God have mercy on your pure soul.

I love you always,

Ed

I read Ed's letter at least ten times or so before soaking it in my soup and consuming it. His words, his secrets, his apology and promise of righteousness would all go to the grave with me. I found it in my heart to forgive Ed. Perhaps I never really faulted him to begin with. In the end, his letter provided me a much-needed peace. In some strange way, hearing that Ezra had faced his tragic, gruesome, unjustified, and untimely death with a sense of honor and grace somehow eased my heart.

I fell asleep with the sound of Ed's and Ezra's voices swirling me into the dream world. In two very different and separate ways, these two men loved me and wanted nothing more than the best for me. The tragedy was, one sacrificed his life to see it through.

10

Forgiveness

I dreamed about Waynesboro the night before my last visit with Francis. The town, its people, the quaint cottage. It all came back as clearly and distinctly as it had been when I was experiencing it. Sheriff, Mr. Dolsan, Branson the shop boy, even Ms. Washington and her son Jordan. No one spoke in the dream; everyone either stared or smiled. There was a feeling of peace and serenity as I viewed the familiar faces, almost as if I could sense the truth of their souls. I could see beyond their humanity, their limitations, the fear and anger that clouded the sunshine in their skies. Despite it all, I saw the good in each of them, a burning peace that allowed me permission to let them go.

Francis and I remained quiet for what must have been a solid five minutes. Sensing the urgency of the limited visiting period, I finally broke the silence with a simple hello.

"We don't have much time, Francis," I confirmed, nodding my head toward the small wall clock that hung silently in the corner of the solemn and lifeless visitors' room.

"Yes, I know," she replied, her voice hoarse and broken with emotion.

"Ya have the journal?" I asked, lowering my head to gain a better view of her face.

"Yes," she whispered, keeping her eyes locked on the metal table. "I'll keep it locked in my bureau until little Billy is about thirteen or so."

She lifted her eyes to mine.

"Is that too young?"

I smiled and nodded.

"That's up to you, Francis," I confirmed, holding her gaze with my smile.

"But . . ." her words faded into a choke.

"It's okay, Francis. I trust ya to know. I trust ya to provide what I won't be able to."

Francis heaved her chest, struggling for air, every ounce of her willpower desperate not to succumb to emotion.

"Just never let him forget about me, Francis. Please. Just please make sure he always knows that his momma loved him and didn't leave him. Please."

I watched as tears soaked the skin of my sister's beautifully made-up face. A river of thick, dark mascara blended into the pink blush of her cheeks as water raced to her jaw and fell from her chin. I held my breath in anticipation of my own tears.

"I'm so sorry, Sista," she sobbed, her head in her hands. "For everything. For the names, the things I did and said. For interferin' in ya marriage and not stoppin' Billy when I had the chance."

"Shh," I cooed, lifting my shackled wrist onto the table and near her hand.

"No!" she shouted, pulling back, alarming one of the nearby guards.

"Ya don't understand, Judy," she continued, lifting her make-up-smudged eyes. "I failed ya, Sista. I betrayed ya in every single way there is to betray a person. And I did it to my own blood. My own kin. The flesh of my heart . . . I have betrayed."

"Francis—"

"I read ya book. Luke made me a copy before sendin' the original off to the publisha'. It broke my heart, Judy. It broke my heart and opened my eyes. I didn't know. I didn't understand. I couldn't see that you honestly loved Ezra, till now."

I didn't say a word as I watched her wipe her face with her sleeve, a smear of a myriad of painted-on colors streaking across the material.

"I'as too wrapped up in myself to see it. Too hell-bent on gettin' ya to marry Billy so I could be close to him. Too wrapped up in old Southern prejudice to see, care, or understand that my sista was simply in love . . . with a boy who was honest and true and treated her right. I didn't see it then, Sista. I swear to ya I didn't. I'as blind."

I shook my head, my throat too tense with emotion to speak.

"This changed me," she spoke, moving her head around the room, her eyes taking in the presence of each and every guard. "Ya gave ya life for ya son. Ya spent five years tryin' to love a man who beat the shit outta ya. Ya did that for Ed, yet for all ya knew he took away the one man ya eva' loved."

I felt a tear fall from my cheek, a parade of others soon to follow.

"Ya taught me about love, Sista. Honest, pure, real, true love. If there is anything that can be gained from all this, it's that you embody love . . . the way it's talked about in the Bible. The way God loves us. The way he sacrificed himself, his Son, and everything he loved for the sake and prosperity of man. Like God, Judy, you love without command. Ya changed me forever."

She cupped her hand over mine, her trembling vibrating my chains over the metal table.

"I pray ya can find it in ya to forgive me, Judy. I promise to live the rest of my life making ya proud. I promise to raise that boy into a man his momma woulda been so very proud of. I promise to do all that I can to honor ya, to remember ya . . . to make right by ya."

The guards rushed the table the moment Francis lowered her head over my hands.

"No touching!" they shouted.

"Francis," I whispered, ignoring the guards as they returned to their posts, "look at me."

Staring into my sister's red and tear-stained face, I said, "I've never not loved ya, Francis."

She shook her head as more tears flooded her skin.

"If it makes ya feel any better, I forgave ya long ago. I knew ya loved me in ya own weird way. I pitied ya anger and sympathized with ya self-loathing. I understood there was a storm in ya mind you were always at odds with. I tried to see beyond the clouds and see ya sunshine. Deep down, Francis, I knew ya always loved me. So there ain't nothin' to forgive now, for I've already forgiven ya a hundred times over in the past. Just do right by my boy, dear Sista. Please, don't let that boy grow up without knowin' of my love."

"I promise," she mouthed, her emotion too strong to allow her an audible voice.

"Please, can I hug her?" she begged one of the guards as they lifted me from the chair, signifying the end of the visitor session.

"No. Remain seated," the guard barked in return.

I didn't look back as I heard my sister sobbing my name.

"I love ya, Sista," she cried, her voice echoing behind me as my chains dragged the concrete floor of the corridor.

Once back inside my cell, I collapsed onto my mattress. The weighted pain of an entire lifetime lifted from my chest as I absorbed the heartfelt apology and regret of my sister. I fell asleep in peace, knowing well that my sister would live her life by the promise of her words today. My son would not only live a life of security in love and family, but he would also grow to know his mother through the truth and actions of his aunt.

"It's number one, Judy," Luke smiled as the guards seated me in my chair. "The press has given it rave reviews. There are all sorts of discussions going on all over the radio and television. You've started a national conversation, Judy. You were right. The truth, the full truth of your story needed to be told. People are connecting and receiving something monumental from it. There's even a group of supporters growing by the day outside the front gate of the prison. They're calling on the governor to grant you clemency. There's hope, Judy. We may still beat this yet."

I smiled, allowing Luke to fall into my expression before continuing.

"There's nothin' to win, Luke," I said with certainty. "The story's already been told. What's needed to be done is done. People now know the truth. However they perceive it may differ, but their hearts have been opened. Perhaps in time sacrifices of justice will serve to inspire great change in this country. Perhaps someday people will be free to live as equals, share their lives as equals, love as equals."

"But this was not a sacrifice of justice, Judy. You were wronged. You were saving your son. You—"

"I killed a man, Luke," I stated matter-of-factly. "I took justice into my own hands, and now I must pay the price for that."

"But the price is too high," Luke argued, his eyes wild with energy. "You don't deserve to die for this."

"An eye for an eye say the scriptures," I rebutted, attempting to ease his nervous excitement with the subtlety of my words and voice. "Make peace with it, Luke. I know I have."

I began to fade as Luke filled the remainder of our time with frivolous details meant to distract me.

"Thank ya, Luke," I said just moments before the guards came to retrieve me. "For everything."

I saw tears fill his eyes as he watched the guards pull me from the chair and into the darkened space beyond the doorway. I didn't turn back and he didn't call out. My last view of Luke Pinder was that of a man broken by guilt, hell-bent in his soul to somehow make amends. I hoped he knew I had already forgiven him.

November 30th, 1963, began like every other day at Mississippi State Penitentiary. The only thing different: I was served a meal of my choice. I opted for a Southern-style Thanksgiving feast. Sliced turkey, mashed potatoes, sweetened yams, dressing, cornbread, and greens. I ate every single bite and savored each and every moment every morsel of food lasted over my tongue. The only time my stomach began to grumble into knots was when the minister entered my cell. He smiled as he sat next to me on the twin-sized mattress, his hands white as he clutched a black leather Bible.

"Would ya like to pray togetha', dear girl?" he asked, his hands trembling slightly.

"Yes, Fatha'. I would like that."

I listened as the man filled the cold, sunless cell with words of comfort, peace, and the promise of everlasting life. I didn't resist the calls for forgiveness as the man begged the Heavenly Father to wash away my transgressions with the blood of a sinless man. I cried as he laid his hands on me, kissing my brow and wiping my tears.

"God will be waiting for ya, dear girl. God always waits for the righteous."

The guards moved in to retrieve me the moment the minister was led from the cell. Silently, they washed my face with a dampened cloth and pulled my hair into a bun. They assisted me into a new uniform and shackled my ankles and wrists for the very last time.

They led me into a wing of the prison I had never seen before, the access doors far heavier and more secure than everywhere else inside the maze of chain-link, barbed wire, and concrete. I could hear a mass of chanting voices as we neared a giant set of red doors at the end of a long corridor.

"Are they chantin' my name?" I asked one of the guards, who refused to speak.

I smiled at the sound. It provided an unfamiliar solidarity and unifying peace.

The red doors opened, and for the slightest moment, I could see Francis and Mr. Jennings and his wife filing into a small door. They didn't see me, and before I could blink, much less utter a word, the door was slammed shut and my feet pulled in the direction of a single black curtain. There was a strange murmuring coming from the other side, the faint chanting of some sort of motor.

Before my imagination could fathom an explanation, the curtain opened to reveal the small door of what appeared to be the entrance to something nautical, like a submarine or a navy ship. I knew immediately it was the gas chamber. It took several minutes before the door finally opened, a vacuum-like suction of air pulling at my skin and hair; a guard appearing with a dead rabbit in his hand.

Donning a gas mask, the man stared at me, my eyes dropping from my reflection in the mask to the lifeless white rabbit that hung from his gloved hand.

The guards began to remove my shackles, the sound of various electronics and motors reigniting around me.

"It's nearly ten," I heard a voice say behind me. "Clemency can come in these last few moments. Still, get her ready."

My heart began to race; my throat hollowed. Flashing images of Ezra, Francis, my mother and father, and Billy Jr. all flickered before my eyes. My lungs collapsed as they led me from the small waiting area and into the chamber itself. A large wooden chair, accented with leather padding and straps, awaited within. I could hear my sister crying from behind one of the mirrored windows.

"Five!" one of the guards announced, the other men busily adjusting the straps that snaked from the chair and around my forehead, wrists, waist, and ankles. The warden stepped before me, his face sullen and still.

"Judith Bracewell, on behalf of the State of Mississippi . . ."

His voice faded into a hollow echo. I couldn't hear him, not even if I tried. I didn't care to. I listened to the sound of my heart as it pounded between my ears, its monotonous drumming somehow easing me into stillness.

"Any last words?" I heard the warden ask, his face now pinched and a bit sinister.

"May God forgive us all," I heard myself say, the sound of my voice shallow and muffled within the airtight seal of the tomb.

The warden retreated, turning to one guard in particular.

"No sir," the guard replied to the warden. "There's been no call from the governa'."

I saw the image of the warden as he turned to face me. Our eyes locked for just a moment, a twinkle of what appeared to be both rage and despair unified as one within his stare. He nodded his head and the chamber was sealed.

The room sprang to life around me, a hypnotic humming filling the sphere. I could sense a movement from below the chair, a soft, lace-like grazing across my exposed skin that began to rise steadily from the floor. I closed my eyes and started to inhale, obliging the suggestion of the warden that I take large, deep breaths in order to speed up the process and achieve unconsciousness.

Clamor. Noise. An interruption to the humming.

"Clemency!" I heard a voice yell, followed by the muffled screams and shouts from behind the observatory glass.

Flash.

A vision of Daddy's face.

Flash.

A pounding and vacuum-like suction.

Flash.

The memory of Billy Jr.'s laughter.

Flash.

Further pounding. The door being opened.

Flash.

A vision of a smiling Ed and Francis.

Flash.

A cumbersome gulp of air.

Flash.

Guards in gas masks.

Flash.

A feeling of warmth.

Flash.

Ezra's smile.

Flash.

Silence.

ABOUT THE AUTHOR

Photo by David Vance

Craig Moody was born and raised in Pembroke Pines, Florida, a suburban community that edges the beautiful Florida Everglades. Author of the acclaimed debut novel, *The '49 Indian*, Craig currently resides in Fort Lauderdale, Florida, with his boyfriend, Gable, and twenty-two-year-old cockatiel, Alley.

To contact the author, please email:
craigmoody@vividimagerypublishing.com